"I can s...
Faye said softly.

She ran her gaze over his taut frame, clothed only in brief shorts, and whisked the towel out of his reach. "You know, Conroy Niall said you were the best bodyguard in the business. A fighting machine."

"I try to give value for money. If you'd let me have the towel—"

"In a minute. There are things I want to know first."

"Such as?" he asked in a voice that held an undercurrent of warning.

"What else does the machine do?"

"Whatever is necessary."

"Does that mean anything I want?"

Suddenly Jason had a disturbing sense of being in another time and place, where he'd met her before. "It means anything Mr. Niall wants."

She flipped the towel over her head and let it slip down to her waist. "But Mr. Niall told you to entertain me...didn't he?"

Dear Reader,

Welcome to the Silhouette **Special Edition** experience! With your search for consistently satisfying reading in mind, every month the authors and editors of Silhouette **Special Edition** aim to offer you a stimulating blend of deep emotions and high romance.

The name Silhouette **Special Edition** and the distinctive arch on the cover represent a commitment—a commitment to bring you six sensitive, substantial novels each month. In the pages of a Silhouette **Special Edition**, compelling true-to-life characters face riveting emotional issues—and come out winners. Both celebrated authors and newcomers to the series strive for depth and dimension, vividness and warmth, in writing these stories of living and loving in today's world.

The result, we hope, is romance you can believe in. Deeply emotional, richly romantic, infinitely rewarding—that's the Silhouette **Special Edition** experience. Come share it with us—six times a month!

From all the authors and editors of Silhouette **Special Edition**,

Best wishes,

Leslie Kazanjian,
Senior Editor

LUCY GORDON
Bought Woman

Silhouette Special Edition

Published by Silhouette Books New York

America's Publisher of Contemporary Romance

SILHOUETTE BOOKS
300 East 42nd St., New York, N.Y. 10017

ISBN: 0-373-09547-3

First Silhouette Books printing September 1989

Printed in the U.S.A.

LUCY GORDON

met her husband-to-be in Venice, fell in love the first evening and got engaged two days later. After seventeen years they're still happily married and now live in England with their three dogs. For twelve years Lucy was a writer on an English women's magazine. She interviewed many of the world's most interesting men, including Warren Beatty, Richard Chamberlain, Roger Moore, Sir Alec Guinness and Sir John Gielgud.

In 1985 she won the *Romantic Times* Reviewers Choice Award for Outstanding Series Romance Author. She has also won a Golden Leaf Award from the New Jersey Chapter of the RWA and was a finalist in the RWA Golden Medallion contest in 1988.

SCOTLAND

North Sea

WALES

ENGLAND

London ★

Haverill Manor ●

English Channel

Underlined places are fictitious.

Prologue

At their first meeting Faye Stafford knew that Jason Royce was the man she needed.

She saw him glance at her with casual interest that sharpened as he took in the details, and she returned his gaze boldly. She, too, was taking in details. Jason was very tall, with shoulders that made doorways seem cramped. His body bore the signs of rigorous training, every muscle tautened to steel, and not an ounce of spare flesh. But a mere brainless hulk would be useless for her purpose, and Faye noted with approval the gleam of intelligence in his cold gray eyes.

She thought she could guess what he was thinking as those eyes flickered over her petite figure and soft fair hair: a dainty doll. Most men thought that when they first saw her, and Conroy had actually said it. "My dainty doll," he'd murmured, slipping the enormous diamond onto her ring finger. "My little fairy

Faye.'' Then he'd kissed her possessively and she'd endured it, smiling brightly afterward to mask her hatred.

As soon as he saw her, Jason Royce knew Faye spelled trouble for him. She was younger than he'd expected Conroy Niall's woman to be, with a fresh, almost innocent face that looked strange with the fortune in jewels and furs that adorned her. The contrast intrigued him. So did the look of frank appraisal she gave him as he helped her from the car. She had a little difficulty stepping out and gripped his hand hard to steady herself. At the last moment she raised her head and looked right up at him out of huge dark eyes. His downward gaze took in the way her blond hair lay against pearly skin, and the swell of her breasts before they disappeared into the low-cut dress. He felt an uncomfortable tightening in his throat. She was alluring in a half blatant, half unconscious way that drew him in against his will.

Faye straightened and he released her hand. She hesitated and briefly he thought he saw an expression of...almost appeal in her eyes. Or invitation perhaps? Before he could decide she'd turned away and taken Conroy's arm.

Trouble! But trouble of a kind that he liked. If circumstances had been different he would have made an approach, but he wouldn't do anything now because that diamond branded her Conroy Niall's property, and Conroy was his ticket back to the land of the living.

"Where did you pick him up?" Faye asked casually when Conroy's front door had closed behind them. They'd attended a dinner with some of his business associates and rivals, and she'd reluctantly agreed to have a final drink with Conroy before going home. She longed to remove the heavy sapphire necklace, bracelet and earrings he'd insisted she wear.

"Who?" he asked, easing her mink wrap from her bare shoulders and contriving to draw his fingers across her silky skin.

"The man who was driving the car," she said, trying to ignore his movements. "I haven't seen him before."

"No, he's new. Ex-police. Left under a cloud." Conroy habitually spoke in short, brutal sentences that he sprayed like bullets.

"You mean they threw him out?" Faye asked, apparently indifferent.

"Not quite. He was 'asked to leave' quietly. Less trouble that way."

"Why? What had he done?"

"Have you heard of Chief Superintendent Wainright?"

"Never."

"The police managed to keep it pretty quiet, but I have a 'friend' in the force who told me what happened. Wainright had his hand in the till in a fairly big way. It would have been very hard to get proof, but there's not much doubt. Anyway, nobody wanted a scandal, so he was retired on a fat pension. Royce was less lucky. He was just told to go."

"You mean he took bribes?"

"Not personally. He wasn't smart enough for that. But Wainright was his chief, taught him everything he knew. When he found out what Wainright was up to he got sentimental. Promised to keep quiet on condition the chief 'went straight.'" Conroy's ferret face creased into a grin. "Can you believe that? Wainright offered to cut him in but all he wanted was a promise. There's one born every minute.''

"So what did Wainright do?"

"Gave his word, of course."

"And broke it, I suppose?" Faye asked wryly.

"Naturally. He's no fool. It was sheer bad luck that the whole thing blew up in his face. Then, of course, it came out that Royce had known and said nothing, and that was the end of him.''

Faye guessed that many of the bribes had originated, if not with Conroy himself, with people in the lower ranks of Niall Enterprises. It was a huge corporation, consisting of several newspapers, a television station and a cinema chain, plus some less openly admissible sidelines. These "small ventures", as they were discreetly known at head office, were small only in that they didn't require large premises and operated in out-of-the-way back streets. They accounted for a sizable chunk of the corporation's profits and any money spent greasing palms to keep them going was considered a sensible investment. Faye knew all this because her father had worked in the Niall accounts department for ten years.

"It's wonderful how you seem to know everything about the people who work for you," she murmured as she accepted a drink from her fiancé.

"Not just about my employees. I have files on everyone I deal with," he said coolly. "The Ennet crowd for instance." Conroy was currently fighting to take over Ennet Publications, a newspaper group. "I hold some handy information about everyone on the Ennet board, and about the people who are trying to stop me getting control. As for Jason Royce—look at this.''

He touched a switch and the rosewood doors of what had looked like a television cabinet drew apart, revealing a computer terminal. He typed something and the word SECURITY flashed onto the screen. It was followed by PERSONNEL and CLASSIFICATION. Conroy typed again and a document appeared. It read:

Name: Jason Royce.
Age: 32
Height: 6'2"
Weight: 164 lbs.
Status: Single.
Parents: Both dead.
Previous Occupation: Police (Detective Inspector).
Reason for leaving: Involvement in Wainright affair.
Special Qualifications: Royce is a trained athlete and tough, skilled amateur boxer. Boxed at light heavyweight for the police. Judo black belt.
Likes: Animals.
Dislikes: Alcohol, tobacco, pills.

"Does he know you have this on him?" Faye asked casually, while her eyes skimmed the screen, trying to absorb everything quickly.

"Of course not. He didn't tell me about himself. I knew all I needed before I ever set eyes on him. And this is only the half. The really important things about Royce are locked in here." Conroy tapped his forehead. "He's as bitter as hell about Wainright, the police and the world in general. That's good. A principled man who's seen the folly of principles is often more useful than a man who never had any to start with."

"Useful? As a driver?" Faye queried skeptically.

Conroy gave his soft, chilly laugh. "Sweetheart, he's far more than a driver. That's just the cover. I've had some trouble recently. One or two people have tried to frighten me off the Ennet takeover. I'm not easily scared, but the shareholders would hate it if anything happened to me. Royce will make sure nothing does."

"You mean he's a bodyguard?"

"That's right. The best there is, a fighting machine."

Thinking of the man's lithe, powerful frame and air of razor-sharp alertness Faye understood this description. But Conroy had missed something vital, she thought, recalling how Jason's eyes had lingered on her, and the way he'd torn his gaze away as if it were an effort. He wasn't just a machine. He was a man whose senses could be aroused swiftly, a controlled man who'd schooled his body by rigorous disciplines, but knew it could betray him. The more she learned about him the more she was certain that a kindly fate had sent him to her.

"Is that why he kept so close to you when you got in and out of the car?" she asked.

"That's right. He was moving so that he always covered me. You must admit he's ideal. He'd make two of me." Conroy never minded referring to his own lack of inches, as though he actually enjoyed being smaller than the men who had to knuckle under to his ruthless methods in the commercial jungle.

Faye had picked up Conroy's hint that she, too, was on the computer and wryly guessed how her entry read.

Name: Faye Stafford.

Age: 24

Height: 5'3"

Weight: 102 lbs

Parents: Mother dead. Father still living.

Status: Engaged to marry Conroy Niall.

Previous Occupation: Dancer with the Kramer Ballet.

Reason for leaving: During performance of jazz ballet *Carmen*, leading man dropped her during high lift. She fell into the orchestra pit and was out of action for three months. When she recovered she'd lost her nerve.

Special Qualifications: A beautiful face and body that might have been designed to show off Conroy Niall's wealth. Bitter as hell toward the damned fool who dropped her, the company who threw her out without giving her a chance to fight back and the world in general.

Loves: Her father.

Hates: Conroy Niall.

Conroy certainly knew all that, including her loathing of himself. He didn't object. It even increased his enjoyment of moments like now, when he could draw her close to him, murmuring into her ear, "You'd hate it if anything happened to me, too, wouldn't you sweetheart? You'd be simply heartbroken."

"Heartbroken," she agreed, trying to blot out the awareness of his lips.

Suddenly his mouth was hard on hers. She endured it as long as she could before pushing him away. Conroy's eyes were gleaming coldly, but he let her go. She could still refuse him, but the net was closing on her. Soon she would be Conroy Niall's wife, and no longer able to say no.

Unless Jason Royce saved her.

Chapter One

Jason paused a moment outside the door of Conroy Niall's office to subdue the disagreeable sensations that the other man aroused in him. He knew it was an irrational reaction. Niall's manner was brusque but Jason preferred that to overfriendliness. Plus his employer was reasonably civil, and the money was good. A hired hand could ask no more. It was just that Jason was an ex-policeman, and Niall reminded him of too many of the polished villains that he'd known.

But those days were over. Now he was trying to support himself as a private investigator, which sounded good but often meant that he was grateful for any job that was offered. He'd protected Niall against a few nebulous threats from the Ennet directors, but now that job was over and he was dreading the lean period that loomed ahead. Niall's message recalling him had been a godsend.

At last he knocked. Niall's chilly voice called, "Enter" and Jason stepped into the office. It was, in his opinion, a hideous room, which accurately reflected the soul of the man who occupied it. The decor was uncompromisingly stark and modern, with chairs of shining steel and black leather, and steel shelving. Even the desk and waste bin were designer steel and had been created to Niall's specification at enormous cost. The walls bore a few abstract pictures, framed in steel. To Jason it was like walking into a strongbox, which was doubtless why Niall felt so at home here.

Niall was standing with his back to the door, gazing out over the panorama of London that lay beneath his twentieth-floor window. He glanced up as he heard the door open and, looking at the ratlike face, Jason wondered what he was doing working for a man who clearly belonged behind bars. Then the curtain with which he'd learned to shut off such thoughts came down in his mind. There was a chaos of misery and rage behind that curtain but he never lifted it; that way lay madness.

"Good, you're here at last," Niall said.

"What's happened?" Jason demanded. "Not more trouble from the Ennet crowd? I had a quiet word with one or two people and—"

"That's all over," Niall said with a harsh laugh. "Your 'quiet word' was very effective. I wish I could have been there to see it."

Jason doubted that. Conroy Niall's kind stayed well out of sight during the rough stuff.

"I sent for you about something else," Niall said. "There's been a kidnap attempt on my fiancée. Perhaps you remember meeting her?"

Jason's mind was suddenly illuminated with a vision of the glowingly beautiful young woman who'd put her hand softly into his and looked up with a curious appeal in her eyes. That look had stirred something inside him. He'd tried hard to forget it but the memory had haunted him, and now it returned, sweet-sharp, making him fearful, as though he'd felt the shifting of quicksand beneath his feet. He breathed in and out slowly and didn't speak until he was sure his voice revealed nothing. "I believe that she was with you one evening, but I couldn't swear to it."

Niall's thin mouth stretched into a mirthless grin. "Most men don't forget seeing her so easily," he said with a hint of relish.

Jason shrugged. "I was guarding you. You had all my attention."

"Quite right." Niall grinned again and lit a cigar. "You made a considerable impression on her, however," he added casually.

Years of practicing facial detachment with the police enabled Jason to suppress all visible reaction. He eyed Niall narrowly, wondering what game he was playing, and demanded brusquely, "What's this about a kidnap attempt?"

"Faye was in her car and stopped at some traffic lights. Another car drew up beside her, a man jumped out and tried to get in with her. Luckily all the doors were locked and she stepped on the gas before he could smash a window."

"It might have been just an attempted mugging," Jason said thoughtfully.

"So she thought until she saw the car again the next day. She's sure it's the same one, and since then she's seen it twice more. I don't believe they're only trying to rob her. Mind you, she's got plenty worth stealing." Niall's grin was half leer. "Like all women her eyes light up at the sight of baubles and I give her everything she asks for. But they can't seriously believe she'd be carrying much in the way of jewelry in the car in broad daylight. No, they want *her*, so that they can demand a hefty ransom from me."

Jason was inclined to agree. He studied his fingertips as an excuse not to look at his employer. Niall's boasting had nothing to do with affection. He wasn't a man to wear his heart on his sleeve. He was saying, "This is the kind of woman I can afford. Take a good look—and suffer." There was nothing personal about it. He would have dangled his expensive toy before any man.

"No one is going to rip me off like that," Niall announced in a hard voice. "I guard my possessions well. So I've arranged for my fiancée to spend the next few weeks at my little country place."

His "little country place" was Haverill Manor, a mansion about twenty miles from London. It had been heavily fortified by the previous owner, an oil sheikh. Niall had bought it a few months ago and retreated to it whenever the Ennet battle got rough. Jason knew its layout and now he nodded. "She should be safe enough there."

"Especially with you keeping an eye on her. That's why I sent for you. Faye and her father will be traveling down there tomorrow. He recently had a heart attack and needs a quiet convalescence, so we're postponing our wedding until he's better. Faye will be able to care for him, but she'll want to get out sometimes. When she does, you'll go with her. Stay with her every moment. Guard her with your life."

Jason studied his hands in silence for a moment more before saying, "Surely this is a job for the police?"

"Faye doesn't want the police brought into this, for her father's sake. She doesn't want him to know anything while he's still weak. Besides, I doubt the police would give her the total protection I want from you." Niall's voice became sharp. "What's the matter? Don't you want the job?"

The question made Jason realize that he *didn't* want it. It might be unreasonable but he flinched away from the thought of Faye and this man. It was all too clear that she'd sold her delicate beauty for his jewels and money, and the fact that she didn't look like what she was somehow made it worse. The lovely face with its generous mouth and dramatically large eyes had an innocence that belied her true character.

Since the wreck of his career Jason was bitterly convinced that all human transactions were a form of bribery. He considered himself a complete cynic, and yet the thought of Faye Stafford in Niall's arms, in his bed, disturbed him unaccountably. But what the hell! She was just another woman, and after a couple of hours in her company he would be able to ignore her. "Of course I'll take the job," he said curtly. "Why not?"

The next morning Jason checked his apartment carefully to make sure he'd forgotten nothing. He didn't know when he would be back. He lived on the edge of the roughest part of London's East End, close to the place where he'd been born. He'd grown up in streets where only the fittest survived and he'd used his fists to get by. He'd needed them because he never quite fit in. The school he went to was a dump, and his peers despised education, considering it suitable only for sissies, but Jason was bright and secretly yearned for the world a better school could have opened up to him.

His mother had been a well-meaning but ineffectual woman whose terror of her drunken bully of a husband had rendered her half stupid. Since as long as he could remember Jason had tried to protect her from his father's blows, and when he was fifteen he'd done it successfully for the first time. He could still remember, with pride, the hate in Leonard Royce's eyes as he stared up at his son from the floor, wondering what had hit him.

It had taken a few more such incidents to make the point, but in the end it had been made. His mother was never beaten again, but she didn't live long enough to enjoy her new peace. The following year she'd died of a heart attack. Jason had stood by his father's side at the funeral and when they got home he'd gathered his things together and walked out of the house without a word.

He had a job as a garage hand, but he quarreled with the boss and left. He got a job in a factory but grew bored. Job followed job, all of them dead-end, bringing in just enough to survive. At night he slept in a derelict house where he and some other kids were illegally squatting. In his spare time he hung around with a gang, looking for something to overcome the aimlessness and frustration of his life, but doing it in an unfocused way that achieved nothing.

Some of his friends had criminal records and, looking back, Jason could see that he, too, was headed in that direction. He made a few court appearances for street fighting and at one of them he'd run into Detective Inspector Wainright who'd seen something worth cultivating in the young tough. Wainright had had a good pair of fists, too, and he'd used them until he reckoned he'd knocked some sense into Jason. Then he'd bullied him into finishing his education at night school, given him books to read and watched him like a hawk, making sure he stayed on the straight and narrow.

Wainright's rescue had been accomplished in a brisk, unsentimental manner that suited them both. Jason could barely remember a soft word from his mentor, but he was happy. For the first time in his life someone was making demands on him, telling him that second best wasn't good enough, that he could do better and was damned well *going* to do better. He conceived a passionate hero-worship of Wainright and at eighteen he'd followed him into the police force.

For fourteen years the force and Wainright had been his family. He'd been a good policeman, hard but just. He'd learned to channel the aggression in his nature into sports and the result was a row of amateur trophies and the respect of men that *he* respected.

Once he'd almost married, but his fiancée had backed off when she realized the strength of his commitment to his job. For a while he'd been unhappy. Then he'd made a spectacularly difficult arrest, and in the promotion and plaudits that followed she had drifted out of his thoughts forever. He'd taken it as a sign that a truly deep relationship with a woman wasn't in his stars, and from then on he'd kept his romances undemanding.

And suddenly it was all taken away. Now, as he drove to Conroy's office, he reflected that the wheel had come full circle. He'd been a rootless drifter when Wainright had picked him up, and thanks to Wainright he was a rootless drifter again.

He arrived just before ten o'clock, and found Niall alone. "You'll need this for expenses," he said, handing Jason a thick wad of money. "Before Faye gets here there's something you should know. I said last night that you'd made an impression on her. I didn't mention that it was an unfavorable one. She's taken an irrational dislike to you, and she'd rather you weren't around."

"You should have told me that," Jason said coldly.

Niall shrugged. "It's just a female whim. I pressed her for a reason but all she could say was that she didn't like your face. It makes no difference. Your job is to protect her. She doesn't have to like you. I'm only telling you so that you can be alert. You stay close to her no matter what she says."

Before Jason could answer, the door opened, Faye swept in and suddenly the dull room was overflowing with life and beauty. Time seemed to stop briefly while Jason took in everything about her, the grace and elegance of her movements, the faint air of hauteur that defied her lack of inches. She wore expensive designer jeans and a silk shirt, and her long blond hair was tied back at her nape. He absorbed all this in one searing second. Then the world restarted on its axis.

"Sweetheart," Niall greeted her with an ingratiating voice that contrasted with his brusque dismissal of "female whims." Jason headed for the door but Niall stopped him with a movement of his head. He put an arm around his fiancée's shoulder and pulled her close to lock his mouth onto hers. Jason saw the way she instinctively put her hand up to push him away, stopped, clenched it, then forced it around his neck. Whatever her reason for marrying Conroy it obviously wasn't love. He'd guessed it, but the confirmation brought a sardonic twist to his lips.

"You look wonderful, as always," Niall growled when he'd released her. The young woman shrugged lightly, accepting the tribute as her due. "How am I going to manage without you?"

"You'll work, just as you always do," she said, laughing. She ran her fingers down his cheek and Jason turned away to the window, wishing they'd finish.

He heard Niall say, "I shall miss you. But I'll come to see you as often as I can."

"That's wonderful." The last word was smothered and Jason guessed that Niall had imprinted his mouth on hers again. He wondered how she liked being mauled in front of someone else. Then he wondered if she even knew he was there. She'd looked right through him.

"Are you all ready to go?" Niall said at last in a more normal voice. Jason turned.

"All set," she replied.

"I've arranged a private ambulance and a nurse for the old man," Niall explained to Jason. "They're already on their way. Faye will travel in your car. Faye, this is Jason Royce, who's going to look after you."

For the first time Faye Stafford deigned to give Jason her attention. Her lovely face was cold. "How do you do," she said formally, extending a hand to him, and drawing it back almost as soon as he touched it.

"I have a goodbye present for you," Niall said.

"I'll be downstairs," Jason said firmly. "I've parked at the rear, where the road is quieter. It'll be safer for Miss Stafford to come out there."

"Wait!" Faye commanded in an imperious voice. Jason turned from the door, taking a deep breath to suppress his annoyance.

"My baggage is in the front lobby," she told him. "The receptionist will point it out to you."

"Yes, ma'am." Jason escaped and went downstairs. There was no need for anyone to show him Faye's baggage. The five pieces dominated the lobby, all Gucci, and all brand-new. Evidently she was making full use of her windfall. That was one very cool, calculating lady, he thought grimly.

When everything was loaded into his car he studied the road in both directions. There were two empty cars parked there. He inspected them but found nothing suspicious and there was no other sign of life.

He went into the rear lobby just as Niall and Faye were coming out of the elevators. Her face bore a discontented frown and Jason heard Niall say, "I can't help it if you don't like him, sweetie. That's the way it's going to be. You're too valuable to take chances with."

Jason wondered how any self-respecting woman could tolerate the way Niall spoke, as if she were a piece of costly real estate. But evidently the Niall millions covered a multitude of sins. He knew that if she'd been his he would have protected her, not from fear of having to pay ransom, but from a fierce jealousy that any other man might touch that soft skin and hold that graceful body with its liquid movements.

She was wearing her fiancé's offering, a heavy chain and matching bracelet, both of which, Jason guessed, were close to solid gold. He wondered if she detected the similarity to fetters, but decided she wouldn't. Conroy Niall's bought woman would be oblivious to such subtleties. He stood waiting at the exit until they reached him, then said, "I'll take over now."

"Surely you don't think they'll try to snatch me here?" Faye exclaimed.

"No, ma'am. I'm just paid to look after you and I'm going to do it. That's my car. We walk to it together and I hold on to your arm so that if anyone grabs you I've got you tight."

"Wouldn't it make more sense for you to put yourself between her and them?" Niall demanded.

"Much more. If you can tell me what direction they'll come from I'll be glad to get between," Jason replied imperturbably.

For the briefest possible moment he thought he saw Faye's lips twitch, but it was so fleeting that he might have imagined it. Niall grunted with displeasure at being corrected, and spoke to Faye. "Have a good journey. I'll be down soon."

He kissed her again and turned away. Jason took Faye's arm and walked her quickly to the car, pulled open the door and stood shielding her body with his own as she got in. As she brushed against him he felt the surge of warmth from her flesh to his own, as heady as a perfume. The air crackled with intimations of danger. She ought to be labeled Dynamite— Handle With Care. He was mad to have taken this assignment.

Jason settled into the driver's seat and locked the door. "That automatically locks all the other doors," he said. "And the glass is unbreakable. No one can get to you here."

"Fine," she said quickly, and was about to lean back in her seat when a sound behind her made her jump. She twisted to look at the back seat and found herself nose to nose with the biggest Alsatian she'd ever seen.

"His full name is Buckingham," Jason explained, "but his friends call him Buck. I thought he was still asleep. Don't worry about him. He looks fierce but he's part of the team that's protecting you—don't touch him," he added quickly as Faye stretched out her hand to pat Buck.

"Why not? I like dogs."

"He's an ex-police dog with five years' service. To him everyone is suspicious until I tell him otherwise."

"You mean he thinks you're running me in?" Faye asked, amused.

"Something like that. When we stop I'll introduce you to him in such a way that he'll know you're a friend."

"And then he'll let me call him Buck?" Faye asked.

"That's right. He's old-fashioned. He prefers a formal introduction at first."

She didn't seem inclined to talk further and he switched on the radio. For the next half hour he negotiated the worst of the London traffic, but at last they were clear of the city center and heading for the south and the Surrey countryside. "Mr. Niall gave me a rough outline of what had happened to you," he said. "I'd like to hear it in your own words."

She gave an account that matched Conroy's and added, "I may have got some of the details wrong. It happened terribly fast."

"Did you recognize the driver?"

"I'd never seen him before."

"But you could tell it was the same man each time?"

"Yes," she said, slowly and reluctantly, he thought.

"You're not sure?"

"I might have imagined that because I was nervous. In fact I may have imagined the whole thing. But Conroy won't believe that. He insists I have to be protected. It's a bore."

"I admire your coolness, Miss Stafford. So there's nothing else you can tell me?"

"Nothing, I'm afraid."

She seemed more interested in looking out the window than in their conversation. Nettled, he said, "Perhaps we should get one or two things straight."

"Such as what?"

"I know you dislike me. For your information, it's mutual. I tell you that so that we can be completely at ease with each other."

She was silent a moment and he had the feeling he'd taken her aback. Probably, he thought, no man had dared say that to her face in her whole life. He was sure of it when she said, "Why should you dislike me? I'm worth good money to you."

"Not everything is measured in good money."

Unexpectedly she laughed, "Bad money then. As long as you're paid, what does it matter?"

"You're not the first person who's assumed that about me," he said grimly. Mentally he filed away the hint that she knew Niall's millions were tainted and obviously didn't care.

"So I should suppose," she replied indifferently. "A private investigator must often get paid in bad money."

"I wouldn't know. I only recently left the police force, and there are plenty of men—and women—behind bars who could tell you I'm a bad man to tangle with."

Her soft chuckle was musical and so incongruously charming that his hands tightened on the steering wheel. "Good Lord, I do believe you're warning *me* not to tangle with you," she said.

To his annoyance he realized that that was exactly what he'd been doing. He stayed silent, determined not to let this arrogant beauty provoke him further.

But she wouldn't let him get away with that. "Do you think I'm likely to want to tangle with you, Mr. Royce?"

"Miss Stafford," he said after a moment, "I'm an employee, you're my employer's fiancée. I'm here to keep you safe and I intend to do it. That was all I was trying to say."

"But perhaps I don't want to be kept safe. What is life without a little excitement?"

"If you think it would be exciting to be kidnapped and held for ransom I can only say that I'm tempted to let you try the experience," he answered grimly.

They had stopped at traffic lights. Jason turned and saw, with a sense of shock, that she'd changed. The chill had vanished from her features, and with her head tilted slightly to one side, she looked at him as though she were sizing him up and enjoying what she found. It wasn't the look of employer to employee but of woman to man, and if things had been different he would have responded. It would have been good to feel her curved mouth yielding under his and to mold her delicate body to his own frame.

But then he saw that she was laughing at him. "My, my," she mocked. "How easily you take the bait. Aren't the police supposed to stay detached?"

It was true, but in a few minutes she'd robbed him of his hard-earned detachment simply by being herself: beautiful, self-confident and provocative. His mouth hardened as he realized that she'd been amusing herself to pass the time. That was what he'd become, a rich bitch's plaything. When the lights changed he rammed the accelerator hard and they roared away.

"So tell me something about yourself," she commanded after they'd traveled some distance in silence. "Why did you leave the police?"

"I don't think that matters," he snapped.

"But I want to know," she said as if that settled the matter.

"And I have no intention of telling you. I'm a hired man and as such I do my job, but that job doesn't include talking about myself."

Faye dropped the subject, knowing she'd gone as far as she dared. She'd discovered what she needed to know: he was attracted to her. She'd suspected it when they first met but today she'd deliberately teased him to see how quickly his temper could be roused. She knew now that his professional detachment was the merest film. If she could break through it one way, she could break through it in another. And that was exactly what she intended to do.

For a moment she wondered about herself, planning her moves in a way that was foreign to her impulsive nature. For the past few minutes she'd been not herself but Carmen, the last role she'd ever danced. But merely dancing had never been enough for her. She had *become* Carmen, submerging herself in the character until she knew exactly how to tempt Don José to his destruction. She didn't want to destroy Jason Royce, but she *had* to make him all hers. He was her last hope.

Chapter Two

Suddenly Faye jerked up in her seat. "Stop quickly," she said in a tense voice. "There's my father's ambulance."

"Where?" he demanded.

"You just passed a pub. The ambulance was outside it. Something must have happened. For God's sake go back."

"I can't turn just here," he began to say but Faye interrupted him fiercely.

"Go back at once, do you hear? *That is an order.*"

Jason breathed hard. "I was about to say there's a roundabout just up ahead. I'll turn there," he snapped. "And stop panicking. Your father hasn't had another attack."

"How the hell can you know?"

"Because an ambulance would have taken him to the nearest hospital, not the nearest pub. He probably wanted a pint."

"He isn't allowed alcohol."

"Then he's probably stopped for an even more prosaic reason."

Jason had been maneuvering the car as he spoke, and now he drew up beside the ambulance. Faye jumped out and raced inside in time to see her father shuffling out of the rest room, leaning heavily on the arm of Don, his young male nurse. "Dad," she said quickly, taking his other arm.

"Nothing to worry about," Don assured her.

Between them they helped Alaric Stafford to a chair. He smiled and patted his daughter's hand. "It's all right, darling, I'm fine."

"You mustn't scare me like that," she said huskily.

"Is he all right?" Jason asked, coming in.

Faye nodded and turned her head away quickly, but not before he'd seen the brightness of her eyes.

"I'm perfectly well, thank you," Alaric announced in his elegant, cultured voice. Jason studied the tall, scholarly-looking man in steel-framed spectacles. He was heavily built, but rather shrunken now, and his clothes hung on him.

Jason offered his hand. "Hello, Mr. Stafford. I'm Jason Royce. I work for Mr. Niall. He sent me along as general factotum, to see that you both have everything you want."

"If it isn't just like Conroy to think of that!" Alaric exclaimed, shaking Jason's hand. "Doesn't he take wonderful care of you, Faye?"

"He certainly does," she agreed. Jason saw that she was under perfect control now, and the smile she gave her father held all the warmth that had been missing with her fiancé.

"I want a drink," Alaric announced, with the tentative belligerence of someone who knew he was going to be refused.

"Orange juice," Faye declared firmly.

"Not that stuff. A proper drink."

"Tonic or bitter lemon," Faye offered.

"Brandy and soda." Then, catching her eye, he smiled ruefully and said with a sigh, "All right. Get me anything that isn't milk."

Jason fetched four soft drinks, then got a bottle of tap water from the barman and headed for the exit. Faye slipped out after him and found him pouring the water into a bowl for Buck. "Sorry I yelled at you," she said.

"Forget it. Being yelled at by the boss is part of my job."

"You were quite right," she admitted. "It was a prosaic reason. I should have guessed, but I'm worried about my father."

"I can understand that. He looks pretty frail."

"But the doctor says he'll be all right," she added quickly, as if trying to reassure herself. "He just needs plenty of rest and no worries. That's why I'm grateful to you for not letting him suspect why you're with us."

"Mr. Niall explained that he mustn't know the truth. Don't worry. I can keep my mouth shut."

"Will you introduce me to Buck now?"

"Sure. Give me your hand."

She did so. Her hand felt fragile in his great fist, the skin like warm silk, the fingers long and slender. Yet her grip was more powerful than any woman's he'd known. He stood still for a moment, savoring the combination of delicacy and unexpected strength. Then he seemed to realize what he was doing and turned to the dog. Still holding Faye's hand where Buck could see he reached down to pat him. "Let him get your scent," he commanded.

Faye brushed her hand across the animal's nostrils and he sniffed her, first the back, then the palm, then the fingers. The dog looked as though he was concentrating intently, getting acquainted with this new creature in a way that told him everything he needed to know.

At last Buck looked up, apparently satisfied. The fierceness had gone from his expression and Faye saw how gentle his eyes were. She laid her hand on his head and he gave her a toothy, tongue-lolling grin. Impulsively she dropped to her knees and put her arms around the dog's massive, muscular neck, and felt the rasp of his tongue and his cold nose against her cheek. She laughed with pleasure and began to run her hands through the thick fur, reveling in the feel of it between her fingers. "He's lovely," she sighed, and was rewarded with another lick.

Jason could see that relief that her father was well had made her giddy. A few minutes ago she'd been filled with dread. Now she was carefree as a child. "When you two have finished your mutual admiration," he observed dryly, "he's supposed to be a working dog."

She looked up, smiling, and he felt again the disturbance within him. It was all wrong that a woman who'd sold herself for dirty money should have a face as fresh and vital as spring. And it was disgraceful that a police dog with three hundred arrests to his credit should be fawning over her as though a light had suddenly come into his life.

"He likes me making a fuss over him," she said.

"Perhaps, but it's bad for discipline. You'll confuse him."

She rose and looked at him quizzically. "You mean what would he do if I turned out to be a bad character?"

"Something like that," he agreed.

"Do you think I am?"

"Miss Stafford, I believe everyone is a bad character, in one way or another. Nothing personal. It goes with my job."

"But you're supposed to be protecting me. Doesn't that mean I'm on the side of the angels?"

"I'm paid to think so," he said laconically.

She chuckled. "Well, you'd better decide soon what you're going to tell Buck about me." Leaning down, she spoke to the dog conspiratorially. "Don't believe a word of it." She turned away and walked into the pub without a backward glance.

Jason watched her go, struck by the gliding beauty of her walk. She had a lovely body, not voluptuous, but small boned and graceful, with legs that were disproportionately long. She almost seemed to float over the ground. "I'm ashamed of you," he told Buck. "What became of your objectivity?"

Buck gave him a brief glance before returning his gaze to the door through which Faye had disappeared, and a soft whine broke from his throat. "I know," Jason agreed grimly. "But she *is* a bad character—bad for us, anyway. I should have run a mile before getting us involved with her."

In a few minutes Alaric emerged from the pub, supported by Faye and Don on each side. Jason helped them settle him in the ambulance and went to wait for Faye in his car. He had the engine running by the time she joined him but she said, "Wait a minute," and began to hunt for her purse. It was brand-new, made of the finest leather, with a gold clasp, but she'd abandoned it in her anxiety for Alaric. At last she found it on the floor. She casually blew off the dust, seeming not to notice that a disfiguring scratch had appeared. No doubt Conroy would buy her a new one, Jason thought.

But then she did something that disturbed him because it didn't fit the picture. She pulled the heavy gold chain over her head, stripped off the matching bracelet and dropped them into the purse. Jason was about to make some mechanical remark about her wisdom in hiding her valuables, but before he could do so she began rubbing her neck where the heavy chain had left its mark, and he could have sworn that the sigh she gave was one of relief.

You're getting fanciful, he told himself.

"Okay, I'm ready now," she said. "Make sure you keep the ambulance in sight."

"I was going to," he said patiently. "Do you have any more orders?"

"Not just now. But I'll let you know."

"Yes, ma'am," he responded with a meekness that was wholly ironic, and was answered by a rich chuckle.

After a while Faye asked, "Is there much farther to go?"

"You don't know the house?"

"No, this is my first visit."

"I think you'll feel safe enough when you see it."

There was a silence before Faye said, "What was that?"

"I said you should feel safe at Haverill Manor. No one will be able to kidnap you from there."

"Oh, yes, of course. Sorry. It had gone out of my head."

"Beats me how anyone can forget a kidnap attempt."

"I have a lot on my mind just now," Faye retorted sharply.

At last the tall wrought-iron gates of Haverill Manor appeared. They were firmly locked and Jason pulled up in front of them, taking out a portable phone. "We're here, John," he said into it. "Open up."

There was a click and the gates swung open. He drove through and when both vehicles were inside he said into the phone, "Okay, close them," and the gates swung together.

"As you can see, they're controlled from the house," he said. "All the trees near the building have been cut down so anyone approaching it has nowhere to hide, and there's an alarm system."

"That sounds just fine."

The house came into view. It was a gray stone mansion, about a hundred years old. The original owner had evidently favored a variety of styles, for the classic lines of the building were interrupted on each corner by round towers. A wide terrace ran all around the base, broken by flights of broad stone steps that led down to the lawns. A middle-aged man and woman were just coming out the front door to position themselves in readiness. "That's John and Martha," Jason said. "They run the place."

He got out with Faye and made the introductions. Martha said, "Your rooms are all ready. Mr. Stafford is on the ground floor and the nurse right next to him. John will show them and I'll take you upstairs."

"Later," Faye said. "I'd like to get my father settled first."

"What's going on down there?" Jason demanded, looking over Faye's shoulder to where Alaric and Don were having some kind of argument at the foot of the steps. As Jason and Faye hurried down they heard Don say, "Sir, if you'd just wait while I get your wheelchair out . . ."

"Nonsense," Alaric declared, setting a foot on the steps. "I feel fine."

Don looked up with relief as Faye reached them. "Miss Stafford, please talk some sense into him. He's set on climbing the steps and he mustn't."

"Dad, don't take silly risks," Faye pleaded.

"I can manage a short flight like this," he insisted stubbornly, and shook her off as she tried to take his arm. But as he hauled himself up a grayness descended over his face and he closed his eyes and leaned against her. Jason saw her stagger slightly under his weight, but then brace herself to bear it. Her arms went around her father in an instinctive gesture of protection, and her face was suddenly wild with fear. Over Alaric's head she met Jason's eyes and he saw it again: the look of appeal she'd given him once before, and this time there was no mistake. She was imploring his help.

"Let me," he said, and took Alaric from her, lifting him easily despite his considerable weight, and climbed the steps. Following Martha's lead he walked straight to Alaric's room and laid him on the bed. He backed off immediately to let Don get to his patient, and Faye hurried to the side of the bed. His last view before leaving the room was of her enfolding her father's hand between hers and smiling at him in a way that was more heartbreaking than tears.

Jason found himself quartered in a room on the second floor that stood at the entrance to a short corridor. Faye was in one of the turret rooms at the far end and no one could get to her without passing him.

When he'd unpacked he went down to the grounds with Buck. The dog regarded the open spaces longingly, and Jason produced a rubber ball from his pocket, hurled it as hard as he could and Buck launched after it, muscles gliding under his shining fur, his great paws pounding the ground like pistons.

Jason kept throwing the ball on a path that took him all around the house. When he'd examined it from every angle they ventured farther afield. The grounds were bounded by a twenty-foot-high wall with broken glass along the top. To the rear of the house was a small wood, covered by the leaves of midsummer. But even here the trees were hung with lights, and between the wood and the building lay the cleared space. Jason nodded, satisfied with the security arrangements.

He returned upstairs and had barely closed his door when there was a knock on it. He opened it, to find Faye. "I came because I had to thank you for what you did this morning."

He shrugged. "Forget it."

She shook her head. "I can never forget a service to my father. He scares me because he's so determined to think he's better than he is. If you only knew how much easier I feel because you're here.''

"Even though you don't like the look of my face?'' he couldn't resist asking.

"Did I say that?''

"Apparently you said it to Mr. Niall.'' Jason suddenly wondered if it were true, or just Niall's mischief making.

But Faye shrugged and said ruefully, "Yes, I think I did. I didn't really mean it, though. I was in a foul mood that day, snapping at everyone. I wish you'd forget it.''

"Sure. Is your father all right?''

"Don says he's just tired.'' She laughed uncertainly. "We got off on the wrong foot. My fault. Am I forgiven?''

He shrugged. "Why not?''

"Shake?''

He took her hand unwillingly. Its delicate feel was as sweet and seductive as he'd remembered. He released her. "I'd like to look around your room,'' he said, "just to check the security.''

She led him down the short corridor and threw open the door to the turret room. It formed three-quarters of a circle, with four large windows that gave a wide view of the grounds. There were two doors, one leading to a luxurious bathroom and one to the corridor. Jason studied the windows, which were fitted with adjustable bars that could be swung back during the day. "Virtually impregnable once the bars are locked into place,'' he declared. "I'll be in to check them every evening.''

"You're very thorough.''

"I like to do my job properly. Fine, that's all I need to see."

Faye showed him out with a smile, but as soon as the door had closed the smile faded until there was only strain on her pale, lovely face. She sat down wearily on the huge bed and contemplated the suffocating luxury around her. This was the room Conroy planned for her to occupy as his wife, and already the thick pile cream carpet and silk wallpaper had the aspect of a prison. It seemed to close in on her as she sat there, warning that very soon there would be no hope of escape.

Conroy had wanted her ever since the day she'd dropped in at Niall Enterprises to visit her father, who was a small cog in the accounts department, and he'd seen her by chance. He'd pursued her relentlessly, inviting her to champagne suppers, which she refused, offering expensive gifts, which she rejected, sending embarrassingly large bouquets to her dressing room.

Then her dancing partner had clumsily dropped her headfirst into the orchestra pit, and she'd awoken in the hospital to find she'd been dismissed with one month's pay. Her state benefits didn't cover her needs and Alaric's salary was barely enough to scrape by on. But the doctor said she needed a long rest.

Even then she'd tried to protect Alaric, struggling to seem better than she was because she knew he couldn't cope with worry. Then, on a day she would never forget, she received a phone call from Conroy Niall. "I'm afraid your father's had a heart attack," he had said. "I'm sending my car to bring you to the hospital. It'll be there in ten minutes."

She had been too distraught at the thought of losing her beloved father to worry about taking favors from Conroy, although normally she would have refused any help from him. She waited on the pavement until his Rolls-Royce appeared. "Where are we going?" she asked the chauffeur tensely.

"The Rydell Clinic," he'd told her.

Faye gasped. The Rydell Clinic was one of the most expensive private establishments in London. Conroy Niall himself had received treatment there. Faye remembered that Alaric had handled the bill and, awestruck, had told her the huge amount.

"Mr. Niall insisted your father should be sent there," the chauffeur had volunteered. "He said he'll explain to you at the clinic."

"You mean—Mr. Niall is there?"

"That's right."

Conroy was waiting for her at the entrance. "It's all right," he'd said at once. "Your father is alive and his condition is stable. Everything is being done for him. I'll take you."

He smoothed her way past nurses and right to the door of Alaric's private room. Then, with more tact than she would have given him credit for, he vanished.

When she saw her father she almost cried out at the sight of him covered with tubes, his face the color of death. His frantic eyes had sought hers, his lips had moved and she'd bent low to catch the whispered words, "Sorry darling . . . did my best . . . made a mess of it . . ." Words that made no sense because she hadn't yet learned the full, terrible truth.

The doctor allowed her to stay for only a few minutes. Conroy was waiting for her outside, and he shepherded her to a private room where he'd ordered tea. "How did it happen?" she asked urgently. "How did you come to be involved?"

"Your father was with me when he collapsed. We were... discussing some of the firm's financial affairs." Faye was too upset to notice his slight hesitation, although she recalled it later. He went on smoothly, "I want you to know that you needn't worry about a thing. He's here as my responsibility and the bill will come to me."

"But why should you do that for us?"

"I think you know why, Faye. This isn't the moment to be proud. Nothing will equal the treatment he'll get here. You won't deny him that, will you?" She shook her head, and Conroy continued, "I've arranged for you to have a room here also, so that you'll always be on hand."

It seemed that there was a kinder side to Conroy. She began to wonder if she'd misjudged him.

For the next week he did nothing to disillusion her. While Alaric's life hung by a thread she lived in the clinic, spending as much time by his bedside as she was allowed. Mostly he lay still, barely breathing, but sometimes he roused enough to squeeze her hand feebly. Once he said again, "Sorry darling... made a mess of it..."

"It doesn't matter," she replied hurriedly. "Nothing matters except that you get well."

"I wanted you to have a holiday," he whispered, "like the doctor said. I wanted to buy you nice clothes and see you happy again. But I got it all wrong." There were tears in his eyes.

"Can you tell me what happened?" she asked gently, wondering what could be troubling him.

"I thought . . . there's so much money, and so many different accounts . . . I thought no one would notice—"

"You took some money?" Faye asked in dismay, her heart in her throat.

"I forged Mr. Niall's signature on a check for five thousand pounds. He found out. He said it would mean prison—"

"Oh, God!" She dropped her head in her hands.

"I'm sorry, darling," Alaric said weakly.

"It's all right, Dad. It's not you I'm angry with. It's Mr. Niall."

"I shouldn't have done it," Alaric said in a defeated whisper. "I meant it for the best, but it was wrong."

Faye clenched her hands, hating Conroy Niall. He made an elaborate charade of courting her, but when he could have shown generosity to Alaric he'd bullied him to the point of collapse. Then he'd played the benefactor, for which he would doubtless expect her to be grateful.

She calmed her father as best she could, and sat watching him while he slept. She longed to call Conroy Niall and tell him what she thought of him, but suppose he retaliated by refusing to keep Alaric in the clinic? Her father was still too sick to be moved, and she knew she couldn't risk it. She had felt the first galling of the golden chains that her father's boss had begun to coil around her without her knowing it.

The next day Alaric was pronounced out of immediate danger, and Faye ran to the hospital chapel to give passionate, heartfelt thanks. As she rose from her knees and turned to leave she saw Conroy standing just inside the door, barring her way. "I've heard the good news," he said. "Which means it's time for our little talk."

"Whatever my father stole I'll pay you back," she said flatly.

"No need," Conroy said with a shrug. "He was caught before he could get away with any cash." He added contemptuously, "He couldn't even do that efficiently."

"That's because he's not used to being dishonest," Faye said.

Conroy grinned. "Unlike me, you mean? Why don't you say it?"

"Both of us are very much in your power while he's in here," she said shortly.

"You're in my power wherever he is, but don't worry. He'll continue to receive the same excellent treatment whatever you do. I want your father to live. Why do you think I took so much trouble with him?"

"I suppose it couldn't have been because you had a conscience about having driven him into this state?" she asked sarcastically.

"You suppose right. Why should I have a conscience about him? Your father is a thief. He deserves to go to jail, as he himself admitted after a little persuasion. Perhaps you'd like to see it."

He handed her a sheet of paper and Faye's blood ran cold as she glanced over it: it was a photocopy of a detailed confession of Alaric's guilt in his handwriting. "I also have the check, which he tried to deposit to his own bank account," Conroy added.

"You bastard," she said bitterly. "He did this because he was desperate. You said yourself you haven't lost anything. Couldn't you have just let him go with a warning? Even fired him? You don't need a confession."

"I rather think I do. I said *you* owe me a debt, but without this you'd never pay it."

"If you mean this clinic—"

"I don't. The debt you owe won't be paid in money. It'll be paid like *this*—" He pulled her hard against him and his mouth crushed hers. She fought him off frantically, and at last she managed to wrench herself away and land a stinging slap on his face. He glared at her, rubbing his cheek. Then the glare turned to an unpleasant smile and he pointed to the confession. "Perhaps you'd prefer me to go to the police with the original?"

"You wouldn't," she breathed, "not now..."

"Why not now? Nothing's changed."

"To hound a man in his state of health," she stammered. "Think what it would do to your own reputation."

"I rather think my reputation would be enhanced among the people who matter."

"Crooks like yourself," she retorted.

"Let's say, people who respect strength. You won't frighten me off that way. I'll turn all this over to the police unless..."

In the pause Faye felt the invisible chains tighten. "Unless?"

"Unless you start being a little nicer to me."

"You mean sleep with you," she declared, her face showing her disgust.

"My dear, how crude. No, I mean more than that. I want to make an honest woman of you."

She backed away from him in horror as his meaning dawned on her. *"No,"* she screamed.

"You should consider it before being hasty. Many women would give their eyeteeth to get their hands on my money. But I've chosen you."

"You can keep your damned money. I'd sooner live in hell."

"But it won't be you in hell, will it? It'll be your father."

"They wouldn't send him to jail," she cried desperately. "Not for a first offense."

"You may be right. Do you want to take the chance? And how would his heart stand up to a court appearance?"

She had no doubt that Conroy would do everything he threatened, but she couldn't face the decision at once. She pushed past him and ran from the chapel, fleeing to her own home. After a sleepless night she arose the next morning red eyed and bitterly resigned. "I'll agree on two conditions," she told Conroy.

"You're hardly in a position to make conditions, but let me hear them."

"First, my father must never know how our engagement came about."

Conroy grinned. "You mean we let him think this is a love match?"

"He must believe I'm doing it of my own free will."

"Certainly. The past few days have thrown us together and you've discovered my hidden attractions. I'll go along with that. What's the other one."

"That you give me his confession and the check."

"It'll be my engagement present," he promised.

"Now."

He smiled but his eyes were cold and implacable.
"My dear, an engagement present should be given at
the engagement party, don't you think?"

They'd stood side by side at Alaric's bed, to tell him
the "happy news." Faye had smiled like any bride,
and her reward had been the lifting of the shadows
from her father's face. She prepared a story to tell him
when he asked for details of how their engagement had
happened. But he never did.

Conroy had begun showering her with unwanted
gifts. He loaded her with jewelry, opened accounts for
her in the most expensive stores and ordered her to use
them. On the night of their engagement party he gave
her a diamond-and-sapphire tiara but, as she had
feared, he didn't hand over the incriminating evidence. "It'll be my wedding present," he'd purred.

But now she knew better. After the wedding Conroy would still hang on to his weapon to force her to
stay with him until he was bored with her.

She'd racked her brains for a way to recover the
damning papers, but all her sleepless nights had re-
sulted in nothing. For Alaric's sake she couldn't go to
the police, and no one else was strong enough to take
on Conroy.

Then, when she'd seemed to hit rock bottom, she'd
met Jason and known that fate had sent her one last
desperate hope. If she could make this man her
champion he could force Conroy to give in.

Faye shivered a little as she recalled how close she'd
come to slipping up today when he'd mentioned the
supposed kidnap attempt and she'd failed to respond.
Her one hope would collapse if Jason suspected the
truth—that there'd been no kidnap attempt. The
whole story had been an invention designed to make

Conroy hire him for her and send them to this place. Here she would have Jason to herself, and a chance to win him over. She'd even pretended to dislike him so that Conroy's suspicions wouldn't be aroused.

She knew she was doing something very risky. Jason had warned her that he was the wrong man to tangle with, but she *had* to tangle with him. She had to come as close to seducing him as possible. The fact that she found him disturbingly attractive ought to have made it easier. But Faye knew that of all the problems she had to contend with, that one was going to be the most dangerous.

Chapter Three

Faye awoke early the next morning. She dressed quickly, rejecting the new, expensive wardrobe in favor of her own old jeans and shirt, and hurried downstairs to her father's room. As she opened the door softly Don put a finger to his lips. He pointed to the bed where Alaric was sleeping and gave her the thumbs-up sign. Faye smiled with relief and backed out.

She went out onto the lawn to enjoy the first moments of the day. The air was still deliciously cool and fresh and she breathed it in with pleasure. She could hear faint noises from the rear of the house, and suddenly a ball came flying into view, closely followed by Buck, racing at full speed. He was a marvelous sight with his brown and golden fur gleaming in the sun. As soon as he saw her he forgot the toy and bounded over, rearing up to place his great paws on her shoulders. He was as tall as Faye, and his grin disclosed a set of fangs that would have been fearsome but for the joy that radiated from him. She slipped her arms around his neck and smiled into his face. Jason came around the corner to find them like that.

He was bare chested and barefoot, dressed only in old jeans, and she could see now that her first impression of his athletic build had been right. He was muscular but not overmuscled and an atmosphere of blazing masculine vitality emanated from him, making Faye's breath catch in her throat. "Buck's really taken to you," he observed. "That's strange, considering he's supposed to be suspicious of anyone who's hostile to me."

"But I'm not hostile to you."

"Aren't you?"

"We settled this last night. We even shook hands," she reminded him.

"People sometimes shake hands over an armed truce."

"Well, this truce isn't armed—not on my side, anyway. I really want us to be friends, Mr. Royce."

He hesitated before saying, "My name's Jason."

"And mine's Faye."

Despite his smile she could sense his uneasiness and knew he was suspicious of her, and puzzled that Buck didn't feel the same. But the dog had seen straight through her original pretence of hostility, and seemed to know she was drawn to this man. If they'd met in another way she could have relished the way the air crackled with excitement when he was there, and the quickening of her pulse in response. It would have been a pleasure to explore his heart and mind, perhaps even his body. She knew just how that exploration ought to be conducted. It must be leisurely, so as to get past the prickly barriers he'd set up around himself. It would take time, but he was worth time, and the rewards would be infinite. This was how she would have liked it to be. But her situation was desperate and she must make the most of the chance she had.

Buck went to get the ball, came back to drop it between them and looked up hopefully. Jason threw it and they watched as he streaked away. "I'm surprised they let you take him out of the police force," Faye said. "Surely dogs don't normally retire when they're obviously in such perfect condition?"

"His condition is an illusion," Jason said quietly. "He seems fit because you can't see the wounds deep inside him. He was badly injured making an arrest. He's recovered physically but he's still nervous, so he had to be taken out of the force. I'm trying to bring his confidence back. It'll take time but we'll get there— won't we, boy?" He dropped to one knee as Buck returned, and man and dog plunged into a joyful roughhouse. There was a lot of growling on both sides and it ended with Jason flat on his back while Buck stood over him.

"Would he do that if you were a criminal?" Faye asked.

"He might, but he'd be more likely to grab me like this." Jason sat up and thrust his left forearm between the dog's teeth. "If he tightened his jaw a little he could hold me. If he tightened it a lot he could break my arm." He withdrew his arm easily. "But he's like a baby with people he trusts. Go on, try it."

She hesitated, her eyes on the great fangs. Jason said quietly, "You have to show him that you trust him, too, Faye."

She knelt and slipped her wrist between Buck's teeth and felt the soft part of his jaw close gently but without pressure. He looked puzzled, as though wondering what she expected of him. Slowly she withdrew. Then, overwhelmed by sudden emotion she put her arms around Buck's neck and buried her face in his fur. "What is it?" Jason asked.

"Nothing," she said huskily. "It's just that dogs are so nice. You can tell them anything and they won't betray you. They don't let you down, they never exact a price and they forgive you everything...." She stopped, afraid that her voice might have betrayed the strain she was under.

But Jason didn't seem to notice. He said curtly, "Yes, they forgive you. We should be going inside. Come on, boy." He began to walk toward the house without waiting for her to answer.

Faye returned to her room to shower and dress properly. Conroy had burdened her with unwanted gifts for this trip, and insisted that she use them. She'd allowed herself to be loaded down with Gucci luggage, but now that the bags had all been unpacked and their luxurious contents hung in her wardrobes, she left them there. When she went down to breakfast she was wearing a cream shirt and linen trousers that she'd bought for herself before her engagement to one of the richest men in the country.

She found Alaric on his feet and looking better. She embraced him warmly, with relief in her heart. "I could eat a horse," he declared as the four of them went into the breakfast room where a side table was laden with a variety of dishes.

"I'm afraid none of this fried food is good for you," Don said, glancing over the display. "But you could have some scrambled eggs."

"Nursery food!" Alaric exclaimed in outrage. "I'm out of the hospital now and the doctor said I could live a normal life."

"With care and moderation," Faye said firmly. "But don't give him scrambled eggs, Don."

"Thank you, darling," Alaric said, scenting an ally.

"Give him boiled," she said firmly.

Alaric pulled a face and Jason grinned. Alaric turned to him and extended a thin hand. "Mr. Royce—our introduction yesterday was somewhat unconventional. How do you do."

Jason shook his hand, then summoned Buck and introduced him to Alaric and Don. Buck stretched out by the window and the four settled down at the table. "How marvelous to be up and about again," Alaric exclaimed. "There's a million things I want to do."

"No," Faye and Don said in unison.

"Don't panic. I know what I'm doing."

Faye's face expressed her opinion of this so graphically that Don and Jason immediately laughed. Alaric looked aggrieved. "The doctor said gentle exercise for a few minutes at a time," Faye reminded him. "We'll take short walks together. And when you're stronger we'll take *long* walks together."

He eyed her with foreboding. "And where do you imagine us walking?"

"On the grounds here. They're large enough. There are trees, and there's a lake we can sit beside sometimes."

"The grand panoply of Mother Nature, in fact," Alaric said, shuddering. "Well, my darling, I'll tell you exactly what you can do with that idea. I am not a nature lover, as you well know. Damned birds always shrieking and dropping things on you from a great height. Insects biting you, miles to go before you reach civilization." He passed a hand over his eyes and the others chuckled at the performance.

Encouraged, Alaric continued. "And the worst of all is people who *are* nature lovers, with their insufferable virtue, always telling you how *wonderful* it is—" his voice soared into a parody of a swooning enthusiast "—just when you're being swarmed by insects. It's my proudest boast that I'm incapable of telling one plant from another, and I intend to preserve that blessed state of ignorance. If I had my way the country would be covered in concrete."

His theatrical manner made it clear that he wasn't totally serious, but Faye smiled at Jason and said, "Dad's a town lover, as you might have gathered."

"And even the town has its disadvantages," Alaric said with an exaggerated sigh. "Noise and gas fumes and people jostling you."

"So what's your ideal setting?" Jason asked.

"A vast library, I think, hermetically sealed against the world. No noise, no people—except my darling Faye—and emphatically no trees, plants or animals—saving your presence, my good sir," he added with a gracious nod at Buck. "Meals would be provided by ethereal spirits who would require neither thanks nor assistance with the washing up."

"Well, if it's a library you want, Mr. Niall has one right here," Jason told him.

"I have the greatest admiration for my future son-in-law, especially since he showed such excellent judgment in choosing my daughter," Alaric said dryly. "But I'm well acquainted with his firm's publications, and I don't think a diet of *Saucy Susie Shares her Sinful Secrets* is going to help me recover."

Jason grinned. "I don't think Mr. Niall would be caught dead with his own publications in the library. From what I saw most of the books are scholarly works."

Before Alaric could reply the front doorbell sounded. Jason immediately went into the hall and picked up the internal phone that connected with the front gate. "Yes?" he said tersely. After a moment he snapped, "No, I'm not opening the gate. Wait there," and replaced the receiver. He turned to Faye who'd followed him into the hall and said in a low voice, "There's a delivery for you, supposedly from Niall, but I'm taking no chances. I'll collect it at the gate. You stay here and don't leave the house until I'm back."

Faye watched him go, feeling a pang of guilt at his concern for her safety, which she knew to be needless. In a few minutes he returned with a small package in his hand. "It's best if I open this," he said. "It all seems innocent enough, but I want to be sure."

He stripped off the wrapping to reveal a black leather box, which he opened cautiously. Inside a pearl bracelet lay on a bed of pink velvet. There was a small card bearing the words, "How I'd like to put this on you myself, my beautiful fairy Faye. Conroy."

"It's perfectly safe," Jason said tonelessly and gave it to her.

"What's going on?" Alaric called from the breakfast room.

"Conroy sent me a gift," Faye said, going in to show it to him.

"He never stops sending you gifts," Alaric observed, taking the box from her hands. He held the bracelet up against the window so that the light made the pearls glow. "My, but you're a lucky girl."

He was beaming. Despite knowing all about Conroy's vulgarity and ruthlessness he seemed pathetically anxious to believe in the reality of his daughter's romance. The truth would be more than he could bear, and for his sake Faye smiled and said, "Yes, I am, aren't I?"

She took back the bracelet and shut it into the box. Jason, watching her intently, noticed that she didn't admire the jewels the way her father had, but seemed almost anxious to get them out of sight.

The telephone rang and Alaric reached for it on a nearby table, and answered it. They heard him say, "Good morning. Much better, thank you. I expect you want Faye." He handed the receiver to her, saying, "It's Conroy."

"Good morning," she said, forcing herself to speak warmly.

"Good morning," she heard Conroy say in his grating voice. "Have you received my gift yet?"

"Yes, it just arrived. It's really beautiful." For Alaric's benefit she added, "You spoil me."

"I enjoy it. You show jewels off so marvelously. Some women make five thousand pounds worth of pearls look like five pounds. You make them look like fifty thousand."

"I thought it might be something like that," Faye said, choosing her words carefully while keeping the smile on her face.

"What a little cynic you are. Anyone would think you didn't adore me."

"How could anyone possibly think that?" she murmured satirically.

"And you do adore me, don't you, my sweet life?"

"Naturally."

"Passionately?"

"Of course."

"Let me hear you say it."

"I don't think—"

"Let me hear you say it, Faye," he repeated with soft menace. "You know how unwise it is to provoke me."

Faye swallowed. "Passionately," she said as quietly as she could, and Conroy laughed, a lascivious sound that made her clench the telephone receiver.

"How delightful to know you feel that way about me," he purred. "We must set our wedding date as soon as possible. Your father sounded really well just now, so perhaps we needn't wait long. Won't that be delightful?"

She knew if he said any more she would be sick. "Delightful," she said. "But I have to go now."

He laughed again. He was still laughing as Faye hung up. She looked around, flinching at the thought of how her words must have sounded to Jason, and was just in time to see him walk out the door.

After breakfast she got Martha to show them the library, which turned out to be magnificent. Books on every conceivable subject lined the high walls as far as the ceiling. The top ones were reached via tall ladders that were fixed to runners so they could slide along the walls.

Alaric breathed a sigh of delight. "I begin to think I shall enjoy this place, after all. Though I must admit, I wouldn't have thought it of a rough diamond like Conroy, but it just goes to show that you shouldn't judge a man from his exterior."

"I should think most of the books were here when he bought the place," Faye said, examining the shelves.

"You can go away and leave me. I shall be perfectly happy now."

"I'm staying right here," Faye told him. "If you want anything I'll get it. Those books look heavy."

She spent the next hour fetching books for him. Watching him, so content and comparatively strong, she felt almost happy. Almost, but not quite.

Ever since her mother died, when she was twelve, Faye had known she must protect Alaric. He was a minor scholar, specializing in myth and legend, and writing books that achieved only modest sales. But with the small legacy her mother had left them, and Alaric's occasional minute royalties, they managed happily. He was a father who would delight any child, with the true storyteller's gift of making characters live. Faye's childhood had been peopled by knights and ladies, wizards and villains. In her dreams she'd slain dragons beside noble Lancelot and received her knighthood from King Arthur himself. Only then did she throw off her armor, revealing herself as a woman who'd followed her lover in disguise. She'd discovered early that to have any fun in days of old it was necessary to seem at least to be a man.

Alaric had introduced her to this wonderful world of fantasy, and it was from him she'd inherited the inner belief that had given such conviction to her dancing. But in Faye, imagination was tempered by a sense of reality that had passed Alaric by. It was she who'd urged her father not to risk their small capital on a wildly speculative venture, and because she adored him she hadn't said "I told you so" when it came to grief.

Failure hadn't soured Alaric's sweet temper. He'd bowed his neck to the yoke and taken a job in the accounts department of Niall Enterprises. "There'll be enough to pay for your dancing lessons," he'd told Faye when she protested, "and I can still write in my spare time." But he hadn't written again, despite her urging. He never would now, but he still dreamed of having time to be a scholar again, and was never happier than when surrounded by books.

Now Faye looked up from her reverie to find that he'd settled on the sofa with a collection of books. After a while he nodded off, and she crept over to the French doors and quietly let herself out. The sun was now high overhead. Somewhere in the distance she could hear the sound of a lawn mower, and the wonderful smell of fresh cut grass reached her.

From somewhere she heard Jason's voice saying, "Stay... stay," and in another moment he appeared around the corner of the house. He was walking backward and talking to someone Faye couldn't see. He noticed her and put a finger to his lips, then beckoned her over. "Look," he said softly, and pointed.

Faye saw Buck sitting in the center of the lawn, his ears pricked, looking around him with an air of tense expectancy. Once he started to rise but Jason called,

"Stay," in a commanding voice and Buck settled back.

"Poor thing," Faye said. "He looks so lost and bewildered."

"That's just what he mustn't be," Jason said. "I told you he'd lost his confidence. He's forgotten a lot of things he once knew. He has to learn again to obey even when he can't see me, so in a moment I'm going to vanish around that corner. The question is, what will he do then?" With those words he grasped Faye's wrist and pulled her around the corner. "Now we cross our fingers and hope he doesn't follow," he said.

From out of sight came the sound of a bewildered whine. "How can you leave him to suffer like that?" Faye demanded. "I'm going back to him."

"Stay here," Jason ordered, tightening his grip on her wrist. "He's got to learn to overcome his pain and fear, the same as we all have. I'm doing this for his sake as much as anyone's."

"But—"

"Listen, Faye, the police wanted to put him to sleep. I stopped that and now I'm trying to give him back the life he's been trained for. He isn't happy not doing his job. I don't expect you to understand that, but take it from me that it's true."

"Why shouldn't I understand it?" she demanded. "Do you think I've never worked?"

"I think you've never done a job that you love, so you can't understand how it gnaws at you to be shut out of it. It's a kind of exile, and it can break your heart." He flushed suddenly as he realized what he'd revealed, and said, "He's had long enough. Let's go back."

They rounded the house to find Buck sitting where they'd left him. He kept still while they hurried over, and didn't move until Jason gave him the signal. Then he jumped up and bounded around his master with evident relief. "Good boy," Jason said, dropping to his knees and patting him. "Good old fellow. You're going to be all right, aren't you? Sure you are."

Faye put out a hand to Buck but Jason stopped her. "Leave him. He hasn't finished work yet. There's one more thing."

He reached for a canvas bag on the ground and twisted so that his body concealed the movements of his hands from Buck. Faye saw him bring out a gun and contemplate it a moment before turning back to the dog. Silently he held out the gun where Buck could see.

At once a terrible change came over the animal. He cowered and took a step back, his ears flattened and his eyes wide with terror. Even through the thick fur Faye could see him shivering. He moved back another step but Jason said quietly, "Stay," and Buck halted. He remained where he was, trembling.

"Stop it," Faye pleaded. "For God's sake don't do this to him."

"Don't interfere," he snapped. "Come here, Buck."

But Buck didn't move. He seemed rooted to the spot, his eyes fixed on the gun. "All right," Jason said at last, putting the weapon back into the bag. Buck stopped trembling but stayed where he was, apprehensive eyes fixed on Jason.

"That was unforgivable," Faye snapped. "Can't you see he isn't up to it?"

"And he never will be as long as you offer him the easy option. It's a tough world he's going back to." He extended a hand to the dog. "Come," he ordered quietly.

At first Faye thought Buck would refuse, but then he began to move slowly toward the hand that Jason continued to hold out to him patiently. When he reached it he laid his chin in the palm. "Why does he do that when you're hard on him?" she wondered.

"I'm not hard on him. It's life that's hard, and he and I are fighting the battle together. He knows that, just as he knows I'm on his side, whatever happens."

She could see that was true. Jason's touch seemed to drive all the fear from Buck. "That's a good fellow," he murmured. "We're going to get there, aren't we, boy? We're going to make it."

He ran his hands through the dog's coat, growling affectionately into his ears, utterly transformed by his love. He seemed to have forgotten Faye and she, too, forgot everything else in rapt contemplation of the deep feeling between the man and the dog. It was a beautiful, almost tangible thing. She knew now why Buck had come to Jason, despite the sternness of his master's demands on him. He loved him and he had faith in him, and because of that no demand would be too much.

She knew how the dog felt. She, too, was relying on Jason, without even knowing him, because her instincts told her this was a man to trust, to hold on to, a big man who, if he championed her, could stand against the world in her defense. And Buck, who knew only what his heart told him, had shown her the way.

Chapter Four

At lunchtime there was no sign of Jason, and no place was laid for him at the table. "He said he'd eat in the kitchen with John and me," Martha explained when Faye queried this.

Faye smiled and thanked her, but inwardly she was disturbed. Her plan depended on her being thrown naturally into Jason's company, but if he was going to keep his distance it would be more difficult.

"How do you like the library?" she asked Alaric.

"I didn't see too much of it. I'm afraid I dozed off. It's this hot sun. We're in for a scorcher of a summer."

"The more rest you get just now the better," Don reminded him. "Also—" he eyed Alaric whose hand was reaching for the butter "—your doctor told me to make sure you cut down on cholesterol."

"What exactly does that mean?" Alaric demanded suspiciously.

"Butter, cream, that kind of thing. But don't worry, Martha's going to get you some low-fat spread."

"For which, no doubt, I'm supposed to be grateful," Alaric said, sounding aghast. "Young man, I was deciding my own diet before your father was so misguided as to even think of you, and if I want butter I shall eat butter."

"Better be good, Dad," Faye said, removing the butter dish before he could make good his threat. "Or you might find yourself with skimmed milk on your breakfast cereal."

"You wouldn't dare!"

"Try me."

"It's a conspiracy," he declared gloomily. "Next you'll be wanting me to eat boiled fish."

"Talking of boiled fish—"

"I give in about the butter," Alaric said at once.

Faye smiled at him tenderly, thinking that if she had children they would probably act exactly like her delinquent father. And for no imaginable reason the idea of children made Jason's face swim into her consciousness. She thought of what she'd seen that morning: Jason, full of rough tenderness toward the wounded animal, the love in the dog's eyes, and a sweet-sad feeling pervaded her, such as she'd never known before.

By the end of the meal Alaric was yawning again. He readily agreed to their suggestion that he lie down but insisted on having some books. Faye collected them from the library and returned to his room just as Don had finished putting him to bed. She settled down, ready to read to him if he wished, but his eyes closed almost at once, and she crept away.

She went to her room and threw herself onto the bed, lying still and listening for any sound of Jason. But the heat affected her, too. Gradually she felt herself growing drowsy and slipping away.

She awoke to find that two hours had passed. The house was very quiet, and she wondered if now she could put into action an idea that she'd had at the back of her mind for some days. She'd heard Conroy speak of a gymnasium at the top of the building and this was her chance to explore it. Perhaps she could start practising her ballet exercises. Since she'd left the hospital she'd tried to practise at home but the apartment was too small for serious work. Her strength had returned now and her limbs were full of tense frustration at being idle. They wanted to stretch and bend, to be full of the old aches and pains that meant they were working to the limit. Above all, they wanted to dance.

She paused outside Jason's room but there was no sound from within, then she went up the stairs until she located the ones that led to the top floor. There she discovered the gymnasium and pushed open the door.

She found herself in a huge, well-lit room equipped with everything a gymnast, or a dancer, could desire. There was a dancer's bar set into a wall-length mirror. One wall had climbing bars, rings hung from the ceiling and the center of the floor contained a pair of high, parallel bars. It was these that drew Faye's attention, because Jason was using them, swinging himself up and around, forward and back, with no apparent strain or effort.

He wore a pair of brief shorts and nothing else. His exertions had brought a glow to his arms and torso and the light that came through the ceiling windows caught the movement of rippling muscles. He presented a picture of blazing vitality and health and Faye regarded him with admiration. She tried to keep her thoughts professional. Jason's physical power and skill meant that he would be ideal for her purpose, and that was all she must think of. But it was hard to confine herself to these austere reflections when she couldn't tear her eyes from the nearly naked masculine beauty in front of her. He didn't seem to know she was there, and she was free to stand and gaze, feeling a soft thunder in her blood.

But she was mistaken. Jason was intensely aware of her. He fought to keep his concentration on what he was doing, but he couldn't shut out the fleeting glimpses of Faye as he whirled past. They vanished in a flash, but they were enough to tell him that she was standing totally still, watching his every movement with admiration and a kind of brooding introspection that he didn't understand.

He'd been about to finish when she entered, but now he forced his tired body on to more dangerous feats, driving himself to the limit. It infuriated him to find that he was giving a bravura performance to impress her, but he couldn't help himself. His muscles ached for respite yet he demanded one final effort from them, swinging up higher than ever and then over into a somersault that took him off the bars to land on the mat. To his relief the landing was perfect.

Faye's heart beat faster as a blinding flash of inspiration came to her. There was so little time. Now she had Jason all to herself and she must make the most of her chance. Her plan was risky, desperate, but it would work if she kept her head. She smiled and clapped her hands with an admiration that he was meant to understand was ironic. "Congratulations," she said. "You're really talented."

There was something in her eyes that made him self-conscious about how little he was wearing, but she was standing between him and the towel. "I work out whenever I can," he said, "just to make sure I'm on top of the job."

"I can see you're very fit," she agreed softly, letting her eyes run over his taut frame in a way that made him redden slightly.

"If I could just get the towel—" he began.

She moved before him, whisking the towel out of his reach and holding on to it. "Do you know what Conroy told me about you, Jason?" she murmured. "He said you were the best bodyguard in the business. A fighting machine."

"I try to give value for money. If you'd just let me have the towel—"

"I'm sure you do," she said, turning aside and speaking half over her shoulder. "You really believe in keeping the machine fully operational, don't you?"

"Give me the towel."

"In a minute. There are things I want to know first."

"Such as?" he asked in a voice that held an undercurrent of warning.

She flipped the towel over her head and let it slip down to her waist, holding the ends playfully in front of her. She faced Jason. "Such as—what else does the machine do?" she challenged him.

Suddenly Jason had a disturbing sense of being in another time and place, where he'd met her before. In that dimension she was a different woman, dark and hotly sensual. But the air of teasing provocation was the same, and so was the sense of danger. "What—what did you say?" he asked, struggling to get his bearings.

"I said, what else does the machine do?" she repeated.

"Whatever is necessary," he replied grimly.

She considered him, her head tilted on one side. "Does that mean anything I want?"

"It means anything Mr. Niall wants."

"But Mr. Niall told you to entertain me . . . didn't he?"

Against his will Jason felt himself begin to tremble. If he'd correctly understood the signals that this disturbingly desirable woman was sending him then a pit had opened at his feet. Thoughts of what he wanted, and what he couldn't have, flashed like lightning through his brain, scorching him with their heat. "Just what kind of entertainment did you have in mind?" he asked huskily.

She chuckled softly and it was almost his undoing. "Isn't that obvious?" she asked.

"Not to me," he replied. "I guess I'm just stupid. Why don't you tell me exactly what you want of me?"

She hesitated just long enough to be tantalizing before saying lightly, "Why, I want you to do what you so unkindly refused to do yesterday—tell me about yourself."

He stared at her in a state of shock. "Tell you—about myself?" he repeated slowly.

"*All* about yourself. Including why you left the police. Perhaps you're a bad character, too, Jason."

He didn't seem to hear the last words. "That was all you meant?"

Her eyes were bland with innocence. "Of course. What else could I have meant?"

As the realization of how thoroughly she'd made a fool of him exploded in his brain a mist seemed to come down over Jason's eyes. Hardly knowing what he was doing, he seized the ends of the towel and pulled them forward, wrapping them around his wrists so that she was pulled hard against him. "Right, you asked for it," he said thickly. "If you want to play games we'll play mine, and see how you like them."

Faye could feel the warmth rising through her body and in her cheeks as she felt the pressure of his hard frame against her. She liked this game too much for safety.

"There's a word for what you are," Jason went on, "and it isn't polite."

She laughed up at him. "None of the fun words *are* polite."

"That's how you get your fun, is it—playing with fire?"

She shrugged. "I haven't been burned yet."

"That's obvious. Nothing's ever touched you or hurt you in the whole of your calculating life, has it? It's about time something did. You might not find it so much fun."

Faye's heart thundered as the hot, nutty scent of his bare flesh assailed her nostrils. Her head reeled with the pleasure of that sensation and it was hard to speak, but she managed to stay in her chosen character, the willful woman teasing a man to the limit, blind to the danger. "I don't think you're the one who could teach me," she said lightly. "And I want you to let me go."

"You announce your requirements very grandly. Suppose I don't do what you want?"

"You will. You have to."

A cynical grin twisted his handsome features. "Perhaps you'd like to make me."

It would have been useless. The body against her was like steel muscle and whipcord. Faye had a dancer's training and could have surprised most men with her tensile strength, but not this man. She met his eyes, knowing her response to his masculinity must show in her face. "You've made your point," she said in a shaking voice, "now please let me go."

"I haven't finished making my point. Your fiancé got it right. I *am* a fighting machine. What I'm *not* is a plaything for you to torment because you've nothing better to do until Conroy Niall turns up to check on his investment."

The blood pounded in her veins, making her breathless as she asked, "Is that how you imagine I think of you, Jason?"

"What else? You're a town woman: bright lights and excitement, with rich men to lavish pretty trifles on you—like pearl bracelets. It must be deadly dull for you here. So what better way to pass the time than experimenting with the machine? Perhaps it's time I showed you how dangerous some machines can be."

On the words he pulled her against him, sliding his arms around her and dropping his head until his mouth came down hard on hers. He kissed her with fierce intent, and did it so skillfully that Faye had to fight to remind herself that she was playing a part. The woman she was pretending to be should try to struggle, show some outrage at the hired man's impertinence, so that he wouldn't suspect he was doing what she'd always meant him to do. But it was hard to remember that when his touch had brought her to instantaneous, blazing life, and every inch of her flesh was clamoring to know him more intimately. She could feel the purposeful movements of his firm lips and it was as though someone had set a torch to dry straw. No other man's embrace had affected her so violently, and already her burning senses were telling her that after this no other man's embrace would do. In one devastating moment Jason had made himself indispensable to her life.

She forced herself to go through the motions of trying to push him away, but her hands wanted to linger on his warm, glowing skin and trace the outline of his muscles. And the feel of his tongue sliding between her lips was driving all coherent thought away, leaving only a void that he was filling with new, wonderful sensations.

Jason felt her fingers on his skin and inwardly groaned at how good it felt. She felt better than another man's woman had any right to feel, but it was too late now. One touch had made the rest inevitable. She was pure flame in his arms, igniting embers of desire and emotion that he wasn't sure he could handle. He didn't even want to handle them. He wanted to yield to them and let the fierceness of the heat wipe out everything that had gone before, leaving only the two of them, man and woman, united by a craving to know each other intimately.

It was impossible to think of her as Conroy Niall's woman when every passionate response he could feel in her proclaimed that she was *his*. Surely no woman could kiss a man like that and not belong to him in the depth of her secret self? And if she was his, then he must be hers, despite all his resolutions to stay detached. He could feel it happening. Her sweet lips had the power to destroy his will, obliterating everything except the awareness of her. And he gloried in it.

Faye sensed him exploring her, slipping his tongue between her willing lips to find the dark warmth inside. The feel of him inside her mouth was wonderful and she moaned with delight as forks of electricity darted through her before shivering into nothing like the explosion of fireworks. He had one arm beneath her head and the other was around her waist, holding her tightly against his bare chest. Her heart beat faster as his hot, exciting scent pervaded her, filling her senses with intimations of danger. This was a man like no other, a man who could bring a woman intense joy or terrible heartache, but whichever it was he would leave her glad that she'd known him. Faye was glad now, with every fiber of her being. If nothing wonderful ever happened again in her life she'd have this kiss to treasure. She gasped and reached for him. It was an unconscious act, as basic and instinctive as reaching for water when she was parched, or seeking the light after too long in darkness.

She felt Jason become very still under her caress. A shudder went through him and the terrible strain that racked him seemed to tremble through her own flesh. Then he seized her by the shoulders and pushed her back, holding her at arm's length. His eyes were blazing but he had himself under control. "All right," he said hoarsely, "that's enough. I don't blame you, I blame myself. I saw all the warning lights about you from the start and it was my fault for ignoring them."

"Jason . . ." she whispered in dismay.

"Leave it, Faye. You've had your little game and found out what you want to know. The answer is yes. Yes, I want you. Yes, you can make a fool of me. Yes, you can bring me to the edge of losing control. *Yes.* All right? Does that satisfy you?''

"Jason, please..."

"I said leave it." He'd grabbed the towel and started to back away, keeping his eyes fixed warily on her. "We'll try to pretend it didn't happen."

She met his eyes. "Can you ever believe it didn't happen?"

He gave her a burning look, then pulled open the door and left quickly without answering.

Chapter Five

Jason began avoiding her. He would check that she was all right and then disappear, taking his meals in the kitchen. In the mornings he collected Conroy's daily tributes but he no longer inspected them, handing them to her without a word and walking away before she could open them.

At night he looked over her room while she was still downstairs and when she went up she found the bars secured over the windows, but no sign of Jason. She would go to bed and lie thinking of the man lying next door, her body tormented by memories of him, her heart longing to know his. She wondered if he was thinking of her.

Once she approached him on the grounds where he was working with Buck, and stood quietly watching them. Buck did everything that was asked of him with growing confidence, but when Jason produced the gun he again backed away, his hair standing up with fear, his eyes wild. "It would be better if you weren't here," Jason told her firmly. "You're disturbing him."

Faye returned to the house, fighting to keep her spirits up, but it was hard when things looked so black. She'd gained a brief advantage, but now Jason was on his guard against her, and she was farther from her goal than when she'd started.

When she reached the door she turned for a backward glance. Jason was stroking Buck and talking to him in a gentle voice that brought a lump to her throat. She remembered how he thought the worst of everyone and wondered if this prickly, defensive man had withdrawn so determinedly from people that he could only feel at ease with the animal. Or might he, perhaps, have a heart for a woman? If so, she felt that woman would be the luckiest creature on earth.

She went to the library where her father usually spent the mornings. But on the threshold she stopped, stiff with horror at the sight of Alaric climbing a ladder. "Dad," she pleaded, "come down from there. I'll do it."

He climbed slowly back down and stood looking sheepish. "Where's Don?" she asked sharply. "It's his job to get things for you."

"I gave him the morning off. I don't like him fussing around me."

"Show me what you want."

"Up there in the history section. According to the catalogue there should be a book called *The Knight And His Lady*."

His air of elaborate indifference told its own story. "Didn't you once write a book with a title like that?" Faye asked, smiling.

"I may have done. The catalogue lists the author as a certain Alaric Stafford. It's always possible that there might be two of us."

"If there are, the other fellow is an impostor," Faye declared. "Whoever created this library must have been a man of excellent taste."

"Get it for me, darling," Alaric begged, dropping his blasé air and looking as thrilled as a schoolboy. "It's the first time I've ever come across someone who's actually bought one of my books."

She was delighted that he'd had this unexpected pleasure, but her heart beat faster as she saw that the history books extended almost up to the high ceiling. She told herself to be sensible. The ladder was completely safe, and whatever happened she must stop Alaric climbing. She put her feet on the lower rungs.

When she was ten feet high she knew she'd made a mistake, but kept going. She was the strong one and Alaric mustn't be allowed to see her weaken, even for a moment. But memory was battering her brain. She tried to fight it off but the world was spinning. She feared to look down because below her was the orchestra pit and her partner's hold was weak; he was letting her go, she was falling down—down—into indescribable pain.

She had frozen, clamped to the ladder. If she moved she would fall, and that was the most terrible thing of all because there was no one to catch her—no one to help her....

She could hear her father calling Jason, his voice sounding distant, then more noises, confusion. She didn't know how long she remained there, motionless, but at last she heard a scraping sound and opened her eyes. The sound was caused by another ladder being slid along until it was against hers, and standing on it, his eyes level with her own, was Jason. "Help me," she whispered. "Please help me."

"It's all right." He reached over and put an arm around her waist. "Now see how you manage." She tried to move but her legs had turned to lead and she shook her head at him in silent desperation. "All right, never mind," he said soothingly. With his free hand he took hold of the arm nearest him and passed it around his neck. Then he reached over to where she was still holding a rung of the ladder, and gently pried her fingers loose. She clung to him. He was the only safety in the world.

Slowly Jason drew her hand across until it was near the one that was hooked around his neck. "Clasp your hands," he instructed her. But she clung tightly to his hand and couldn't force herself to let go. "You must," he said. "I promise you I know what I'm doing." He smiled into her eyes. "It's not that hard to trust me, is it?"

"You're the only person I *can* trust," she whispered. "If it wasn't for that..." She drew in a long, shuddering breath.

Jason stared. There was something in her voice and her eyes that touched his heart, something that went beyond this situation. But there was no time to think of it now. He held her gaze, almost hypnotizing her while he eased her two hands closer until she could clasp them together. Then he tightened his arm around her waist and pulled her toward him, lifting her slightly so that her feet left the ladder. With her body held tightly against his he began to descend.

She was trembling when he reached the floor and he had to fight an impulse to pull her against him and promise to shield her from whatever strange terror had attacked her, promise to shield her from everything. But her father was watching them, so he carried her to the nearest chair. She was a ghastly color.

Alaric hovered uneasily around his daughter. "Darling, I'm so sorry. I shouldn't have let you, but I didn't realize... I've been so wrapped in my own troubles that I forgot..."

"It's all right, Dad," she interrupted him quickly. "It was just a little dizzy spell. I'm fine."

Her heart was beating fast. Alaric had come close to blurting out the secret that Jason mustn't suspect—not yet. She reached up to put a hand on her father's shoulder and smiled reassuringly at him.

Jason had barely heard Alaric's confused words. His eyes were fixed on Faye's face, watching the strain that was still there although the smile covered it like a mask. He wondered if Alaric could see through the mask as clearly as he could himself. Abruptly he walked out of the room.

He wanted to go far away, anywhere where he could forget the sensation of her body against his, reviving forbidden memories that he'd sworn to suppress. He wanted to deny the way his flesh was aching to explore her more fully and discover how she'd feel if there were no barriers between them. For two nights he'd lain wakeful and confused, trying to drive away her image, but now she'd done something for which he'd been unprepared and had no defenses, and which had filled him with a sense of danger.

It wasn't the way she'd clung to him so that he could feel the intoxicating soft warmth of her flesh through her clothes. It was the way she'd looked into his eyes and told him with such heartbreaking intensity that he was the only person she could trust.

Later that afternoon, encountering Jason by chance, Alaric demanded to know if he could play chess. On hearing that he could he requested him for the evening. After supper they repaired to Alaric's room and settled down to some serious play. Jason wondered if Faye would join them, but to his confused relief and disappointment she vanished upstairs.

He was no mean player, but he soon realized he was going to be soundly beaten. He was. "I guess you've done it again," he said ruefully after the third time.

"Naturally. I cheat," Alaric declared with childlike glee.

"Damned if I can tell how."

"If you could tell how there'd be no point. Let's have another game, and see if you can spot it this time."

Jason was about to agree when the door opened and Faye walked in. She was wearing a dress of deep blue silk that emphasized the vivid blue of her eyes, and her feet were adorned by delicate silver sandals. Like everything else about her appearance they proclaimed that she wasn't planning to spend the evening sedately indoors. "I'm going out, Dad," she said cheerfully.

"At this hour?" he queried. "It's nearly nine o'clock."

"What better time to explore a new town?" she said lightly. "Cranton is a reasonably big place. There must be some excitement going on somewhere."

"Must you have excitement? What's wrong with a quiet evening at home?"

"*Too* quiet." Faye shot a brilliant look at Jason as she added, "I'm a town woman. I like bright lights. So I'm going to find them."

Jason gave her a wry look but said nothing.

"Gadabout," Alaric chided her cheerfully. "Have a nice time, darling."

Jason moved quietly away as Faye went over to kiss her father, and when she left the room he was waiting for her in the hall. "Exactly where are you going?" he asked.

"Just into town. I'll try to find a nice restaurant, and then look around."

"Fine, just give me a minute to change my clothes."

"No, not us—just me. I don't fancy being hampered by a companion."

"And I don't fancy having to explain to Mr. Niall how you were kidnapped because I let you go out alone."

"Oh, nonsense! Nobody knows I'm here. Have you seen any sinister strangers lurking around?"

"No, but my orders were to go with you whenever you left the house—I'll be as quick as I can getting ready."

"I'm not waiting for you," she said, looking cross. "I'm going now, and I'm going alone."

"Do you want to bet on that?"

She shrugged and turned toward the front door, but before she could reach it Jason said quietly, "Stop her," and suddenly Buck was there in her path. When she tried to push him gently aside he seemed to take root in the floor.

"Good boy, let me pass," she coaxed. He wagged his tail, but didn't budge. "Come on, old fellow. It's me. We're friends."

He thrust his chin into her hand in eager confirmation, but stayed where he was. Faye tried to walk around him but he moved to head her off. She tried in the other direction but again he intercepted her. She began to feel like a sheep being rounded up. "Very funny," she said indignantly in answer to Jason's grin.

"Guard the door," he ordered and vanished upstairs. Buck promptly went to the front door and stretched out in front of it.

"If you think I'm scared of you..." Faye exclaimed.

He looked hurt. His tail thumped once as if to say he wasn't trying to scare her.

"I know very well you wouldn't harm me and I'm going to unlock that door."

She had a momentary qualm as she reached over Buck's head, but as she'd guessed, he was harmless to her. He lay still as she undid the lock and opened the door a crack. And he continued to lie still as she tried vainly to pull it wider against ninety pounds of stubborn, determined dog. "Buck!" she exclaimed, half laughing, half exasperated.

His tail thumped the floor again but his eyes were puzzled as if to ask why she was being so unreasonable.

Faye glanced up the stairs to make sure Jason was out of earshot, then dropped to her knees and whispered, "You're not fooled, are you? You know I meant him to come with me all the time."

She'd guessed that a direct invitation would put Jason on his guard, so she'd hit on the idea for the lit-

tle comedy of reluctance that she'd just played. It had
worked better than she'd dared hope. She went and
put her head around Alaric's door. "I'm afraid you've
lost your opponent for tonight, Dad. Jason feels he
should escort me."

"Perfectly right. A young woman shouldn't go out
alone these days. Too many muggers."

She left Don settling Alaric for the night and returned to the hall where Buck hadn't relaxed his
guard. At last Jason came downstairs wearing a dinner jacket. "Will I do?" he asked ironically.

Her heart skipped a beat at how handsome he
looked. She was used to seeing him casual and tou-
sled, but the elegant clothes gave him a new, intrigu-
ing dimension. Beneath them the hard lines and lithe
movements of his body were tantalizingly revealed. "I
see you come prepared for anything," she replied
lightly. "If this is how it has to be I guess I must accept it."

"All right, Buck, at ease," Jason directed.

Buck moved away from the door at once and nuzzled Faye. She scratched his head to show there were
no hard feelings.

It was twilight as Jason escorted her to the car. He
kept every sense alert, not for fear of outside attack
but because he'd learned that with Faye he must be
ready for the unexpected. Already he was troubled by
a sense of something about her being just off-key, but
he hadn't time to analyze it.

The evening air was soft and balmy, the last whisper of a perfect summer day. Faye wound down the
window and leaned back pleasurably. "Did you have
anywhere special in mind?" he asked as he started the
engine.

"I've never been to Cranton before. All I know is I wanted a change of scene. I leave the details to you since you're determined to supervise every second of my life." She managed to sound aggrieved.

"Look, Faye, my orders are to stay with you."

"And you just hate the orders, don't you?"

After a moment he said, "You know better than that."

When they had driven in silence for a while she said, "I ought to thank you for rescuing me this morning."

"Are you all right now?"

"Oh, yes, I'm fine. I feel silly making such a fuss. That ladder wasn't so very high."

"Well, I guess we never know what'll happen to us unexpectedly," he observed.

"That's true. Life always seems to pull the rug out from under you just when you thought you were doing all right."

"I shouldn't worry," he said cynically. "Your rug is safe enough."

"I beg your pardon?"

"Sapphire earrings this morning, wasn't it?"

"No, solid gold," she said coldly. "Sapphires were yesterday."

After that they said no more until they reached town.

Cranton was a fairly large, prosperous town about five miles away. Jason drove through it slowly, looking around him until he spotted what looked like a quiet restaurant. "Let's go there."

He parked at the rear and they made their way inside. They were shown downstairs and at once Faye realized the quiet exterior was deceptive. The tables were grouped around a dance floor, and through a nearby arch she could see a crowd under glittering lights. The waiter showed them to a table, offered them drinks and raised his eyebrows in supercilious displeasure when they both chose orange juice. "He probably thinks we've got a screw loose," Jason observed.

"I'm not surprised," Faye said, studying the crowd through the arch. Their backs were turned to the main room and they seemed absorbed in something beneath them. Occasionally a man's voice cracked above the general hum. "You've brought us to a casino."

"Is that what's through there? This is supposed to be a sedate evening. Let's find someplace else."

"Oh, stop being a policeman for five minutes," she chided, shaking his hand off. "I want to have a look. I've never been anywhere like this before."

Jason shot her a wry look, wondering who she thought she was fooling. It just wasn't credible that the kind of woman she was had never gambled in a casino.

But suddenly it dawned on him why he'd been troubled by her this evening. She *looked* wrong. As a man who'd had a lot of stolen valuables pass through his hands, Jason could cost many things on sight. That blue chiffon dress that swirled around the most slender and shapely calves he'd ever seen—it was attractive but not luxurious, and it had not been bought by her millionaire fiancé. And neither had the simple silver pendant around her neck. Style and elegance emanated from the woman herself.

In the same moment as he realized all this, he knew that he hadn't the slightest idea what kind of woman she really was—and that it mattered to find out.

Faye had risen and gone toward the gaming room without looking to see if Jason was following. She bought some chips and took a place at the table. After a moment he came to stand behind her. The croupier asked where she wanted to place her bet and she cautiously laid a pound chip on red ten. The wheel spun and when it slowed the ball was in black sixteen. Faye immediately laid five pounds on black thirty. She'd never gambled before but once she'd started it came naturally. She had an odd sense that everything else in her life had been suspended, and only the wheel was real.

She lost four times and then got lucky and won a hundred pounds. Her spirits soared wildly as she reached for her winnings. In her hands was tangible proof that she could gamble and win. Now anything could happen. Even the gamble in her life could pay off. She placed another stake.

After ten minutes there was nothing left of her winnings, but her mind vehemently rejected the implications. She had won and could win again. She continued to play intently and in a few minutes had also lost the money she started with. "I'll get you some more chips," Jason said.

She watched him take a wad of money out of his pocket and hand over two fifties without blinking. "You can't afford that," she said. "I don't want you paying for me."

"Don't worry, I'm not. Mr. Niall gave me plenty for expenses."

He was startled by the fierce look that came into her eyes. Without a word she rose and pushed past him to get to the booth, where she produced her credit card. "Fifty pounds worth," she said recklessly, wondering if she had that much left. In a moment fifty pounds worth of chips were in her hand and she made her way back to the table.

"What's wrong with these?" Jason demanded, indicating the chips he'd brought her.

"I prefer my own," she said.

"I've told you, your fiancé bought these—" he began.

"I know, and I don't want them."

"But—"

"No," she said fiercely.

Jason stared at her but said no more.

At the table Faye was clenching and unclenching her hands. To have another win and restore her lucky streak had become the most important thing in the world. Taking a deep breath she staked the whole fifty on one number. A minute later it was gone.

Suddenly she was frantic. She'd thrown her good luck away and if she didn't get it back at once it would be lost forever. She jumped up and began to make her way to the seller, drawing her credit card out as she went.

"Faye!" Jason had gotten in front of her and taken her by the shoulders. "That's enough."

"Get out of my way," she said tensely.

He stared into her face, and the look of recklessness bordering on hysteria he saw there disturbed him. He wondered if she was a compulsive gambler, but her rejection of Conroy's money didn't fit the picture. What was clear was that she'd slipped into another dimension, one where she found no peace. "Come on," he said, trying to guide her away.

She pulled her arm away. "I've got to go on," she said. "You don't understand."

The burning intensity in her eyes told him it was useless reasoning with her. Somewhere behind him he could hear music starting up. He grasped Faye's wrist and walked away, giving her no choice but to follow, and didn't stop until he'd reached the dance floor. Before she knew what was happening Faye felt his arm around her waist and he whirled her across the floor at great speed. Her dancer's limbs responded instinctively and for several minutes she could do nothing but follow his lead. Jason surprised her by being an excellent dancer, and when he became adventurous she had to concentrate to keep up with him.

The music changed to a slow waltz. Jason held her tighter and kept dancing. "What got into you?" he demanded.

"I don't know. The devil perhaps."

"I think the devil was born in you," he growled. "Or perhaps it's an angel. I never know."

She laughed up at him recklessly. The gambling fever had spent itself, only to be replaced by another kind that was even more heady. She felt suspended in time and space because she was in Jason's arms.

"What got into you?" he demanded.

"I wanted to win."

"Then you should have staked your fiancé's money."

"It's not the same. *I* had to win. Not Conroy, *me*."

His mouth twisted. "But surely 'man and wife are one flesh'?"

"I'm not Conroy's wife yet," she said vehemently.

"As near as makes no difference. Don't forget what a catch he is."

"Ah yes, I'm the luckiest woman in the world, aren't I? I'm engaged to a man who adores me and sends me expensive gifts every day."

He thought he understood. "So you wanted to make a little money of your own? But you went about it the wrong way. You can't win by staking everything on one number."

"Sometimes that's the only way to win. You should have left me there. I'd have got lucky again."

"No, you wouldn't. The odds are always against you."

"I make my own odds. Do you think I can't?"

"I think," he said slowly, "that you could do anything you set your mind to, and that worries me. I should escape you while I can."

She smiled. "Am I bad for you, Jason?"

"Yes," he said simply.

"Then escape me now."

"I can't," he murmured, looking down into her eyes. They were like mysterious pools that seemed to invite him into their depths. He could feel the beat of his heart, warning him of the powerful spell she cast, a spell in which he was growing more entangled every minute.

He thought of the call he'd tried to put through to Conroy that afternoon, to say he wanted to be relieved of this assignment. Conroy hadn't been available, and Jason knew now that another call would never be made. The sight of her lovely face held him, making it impossible to look away. As if drawn by a magnet he lowered his head until their lips were a whisper apart. In another moment they would be touching and he wanted it to happen.

Abruptly the music came to an end. He heard her little sigh as she returned to reality. They looked at each other, suddenly self-conscious. "It's time we had something to eat," Jason said.

He led her back to their table, keeping hold of her hand. The waiter reappeared and Faye ordered steak, salad and mineral water. "Not champagne and caviar, please note," she said with a teasing glance at Jason.

"All right," he conceded. "I admit I jumped to conclusions about you, although you had some fun letting me jump, didn't you?"

His eyes held hers, challenging her to make a direct reference to what had happened in the gym. She smiled. "Let's just say I resented your assumption that I'd sold myself to a man, body and soul, just because he could give me a few jewels. Whatever it looks like, I'm my own woman, Jason."

"Does Conroy Niall know that?" he asked wryly.

"If he doesn't it's his own fault. But sometimes being your own person has to be a private thing. On the outside you can seem a prisoner and your independence becomes something you must cherish inside."

He stared at her, thunderstruck. It was as though she'd looked into his mind and spoken his thoughts. In the bitter months since the ruin of his career he'd clung to the thought that his soul was still his own, the last possession left in a world that had stripped him of everything else. And she knew that feeling. Looking into her clear eyes he suddenly realized that the shallow woman he'd despised was a creature of his imagination. She had depths that could take a man all his life to reach. She smiled at him, a slow, sweet smile that seemed to welcome him into her warmth. "I was thrown out of the police," he said abruptly. "They said I was corrupt and asked me to go quietly."

"But you're not corrupt, Jason," she said. It was a plain statement of fact, without question or doubt, and he felt a twinge of half incredulous pleasure at her belief in him.

"No, but I was guilty by association. That can be the worst kind of guilt because you can't fight it. My chief was taking kickbacks from drug dealers. When I first began to suspect that, I refused to accept it. Don was practically a father to me. He'd picked me up when I was a street-smart kid who could have gone either way. I thought I was tough but he was tougher, and in those days toughness was the only thing I respected. Don straightened me out and made me believe in myself. I joined the police because I hero-worshiped him.

"The hero-worship didn't last. I grew up and started to see him as he was—or as I thought he was: fallible but basically decent and straight. I didn't have any family of my own, except for my real father, whom I don't consider as family, but I always knew I could go to Don's house and his wife, Clarry, would say, 'Gotta feed you up, boy,' and put a huge plate of ham and eggs in front of me. When I was promoted we all celebrated together.

"Then I arrested a drug dealer, not one of the little guys, the kind that usually get picked up, but someone who really counted. I thought I'd got lucky, but it was the start of a nightmare. The man said there'd been a mistake. He shouldn't be touched because he'd 'paid his dues.' When I heard who he'd paid them to—" Jason broke off and closed his eyes, shaking his head as if still disbelieving the memory.

After a moment he looked up at Faye. He smiled, but it was a twisted smile full of bitterness. "According to him Don was feathering his nest with bribes, in return for looking the other way when it mattered," he said softly. "I went to Don, almost begging him to deny it. He spun me a sob story about how Clarry was sick and she needed expensive private treatment. I fell for it, but I told him it had to stop now if he wanted me to forget what I knew.

"He tried to change my mind, said he'd cut me in. I should have seen the warning lights then. I suppose in a way I did, but I still wanted to trust him because—" Jason sought for the words "—if he was a 'wrong one,' then everything was wrong, and the way I'd believed in him for years was nothing but a sick joke. Well, I paid the price for being sentimental. The trouble is, so did other people."

"What happened?" Faye asked gently.

"He asked for breathing space, just a few days to do some thinking. I agreed because I was so sure I was going to win in the end. Then I got a tip-off about a big shipment of cocaine. I arranged a major operation at the docks, undercover men, sniffer dogs, the lot."

He stopped, apparently unwilling to go on. Faye took his hand. "Was Buck one of the dogs?" she asked.

"Yes," he said heavily. "You should have seen him in those days, Faye, the finest animal on the force. I knew him well because Harry, his handler, was a good friend of mine. As well as working they were in the display team, giving exhibitions at shows. Buck has a cupboard full of cups and rosettes, plus a decoration for saving a child's life, and more honorable mentions in police files than I could count. He was one of the first dogs I asked for when it was a big job.''

"Did things go wrong?"

"Go wrong? It was a setup. There was no cocaine, nothing except men waiting for us with guns. One of them tried to shoot me, but Buck leaped at him. He caught the bullet that was meant for me. I came out of it unscathed, which was the biggest joke of all, seeing that I was the one they really wanted to get."

"You mean...?" Faye breathed, hardly able to take in the horror of what he was telling her.

"I mean Don was behind it. That's how he'd used the breathing space I gave him."

"He tried to kill you?" she said in incredulous horror.

"It was necessary from his point of view. Since he couldn't buy me I was dangerous and had to be put out of the way. But one of the undercover men got a hint of what Don was up to, and he did what I should have done in the first place: went straight to headquarters. Don was called in for questioning but he'd been clever. There was no proof, just a very strong presumption. He was thrown out and before he went he managed to throw just enough mud at me to stick. I had to admit I'd discovered what he was doing and not reported it. That finished me.

"What hurt the most was Buck. When I saw him fighting for his life, blood pouring out of a great hole in his side I nearly cried. He was taken to a vet, and he recovered, but he'd lost his nerve. He'd been close enough to see the gun that shot him and now he can't bear the sight of one. He's useless to the police and they wanted to put him down. They said he was unpredictable and might turn dangerous, but I know him better than that." Jason gave a slight shrug. "So I stole him."

"Good for you," Faye said at once.

"I had a bit of help. The man in charge of Buck didn't want him to die either. So he managed to be a bit careless, and when he discovered him missing he reported that he'd escaped. It was something I just had to do. I feel as though I put that bullet into Buck. It wouldn't have happened if I'd spoken up sooner."

"Buck doesn't blame you," Faye said. "He loves you."

"I know. That hurts too in its own way. But if I can make him as good as he was . . ."

She took his hand between both hers. "It'll ease the load of guilt you carry, won't it?" she said softly.

"Yes, that's it." He could hardly believe how good it felt to have his great fist resting between her delicate fingers. Her touch was gentle and reassuring, and looking into her eyes he knew that she understood the burden he carried. For the first time in months a feeling of peace came over his heart. There was still hope in the world. He hadn't discovered it yet, but it was there, and this gentle, compassionate woman could show him the way to find it.

It was impossible to connect what she seemed to be with what his heart told him about her, and now he knew that the truth wasn't to be found in the trappings of her situation, that the jewels and luxury had blinded him too long, and behind them the real woman was waiting for him to see her clearly. He must throw away all his preconceived ideas and start again from the beginning.

As if from a great distance, he heard music start to play again. "Dance with me, Faye," he said. "I want to hold you close."

Without a word she rose. Still hand in hand they went onto the floor. He opened his arms and she went into them as if in a dream.

Chapter Six

The lights were low as they danced, covering them in a haze through which Faye could dimly see Jason. But she didn't need sight. She could feel the warmth of his body and hear his breathing close to her ear, and in the semidarkness there was just the two of them and nothing else in the world.

Happiness flooded her because he had confided in her, trusting her enough to reveal his wounds. It was as though he had opened his arms to invite her in, and this gave her even more joy than the close physical embrace in which he held her.

She knew they'd discovered each other in a new way tonight. It was what she wanted, but she had no need to feel guilty. What was happening between them wasn't a part of her scheme. While listening to Jason her heart had ached for his tragedy, and she'd forgotten that she ever had a plan to win him over. She was a woman sharing a moment of intimacy with a man to whom she was strongly drawn, a man she knew she could love, and who might come to love her. She had seen and understood the surprise in Jason's eyes as he found himself talking about his deepest pain. She could guess how little tenderness there had been in his life, and his confusion at its unexpected dawning with her. She longed to make that tenderness flower, not for her own sake but for his.

"Look at me, Faye," he whispered.

She looked up and at once he bent his head and put his lips gently to hers. The touch was feather light, but she felt it at once, and instinctively molded her body to his, caressing his lips with her own. "Faye..." He breathed her name so softly that only her heart heard.

The music was slow and languorous. She gave in to it in blissful content, enjoying the movements of Jason's body against her own. For Faye, movement was poetry and her chosen language. She had thought she knew all the subtle communications it could make. But now she found that their instinctive physical rapport had a thousand new things to teach her. None of her professional partners had revealed how a man and woman could unite in perfect sympathy, until it was unclear where one ended and the other began. But she knew every feeling that was possessing Jason because the same feelings possessed her. She shared with him the secret quickening of the blood, the excitement running over the skin and the sense of unutterable wonder that this miracle could actually be happening.

"What is it?" Jason asked urgently.

"What do you mean?"

"You sighed, but it was to yourself, as though you didn't want me to hear."

"I didn't know I sighed."

"What's wrong?"

"I was a little sad because I so much want this to last for ever, and I know it can't."

His lips were very close to her ear. "Perhaps you're wanting the wrong thing. Perhaps life has something better in store for us, and we'd miss it if tonight lasted forever."

"No, hush!" she said with sudden fearful urgency. "Don't look to the future. Don't ask for more. Let's just be glad of this while we have it."

She felt as though someone else were speaking through her. She had always meant to ask for Jason's help against Conroy as soon as she sensed him inclining toward her. But now that the moment had come, she couldn't bear to put the brutal truth into words, and break the spell they'd created between them. Let tonight last a little longer, her heart entreated, and she would tell him later, when he was more completely hers. Surely that was good sense? Somewhere in the universe the voice of reason mocked her, but she couldn't hear it. She couldn't hear anything but the slow thunder of Jason's heart mingling with her own.

"You're right," Jason said. "We shouldn't question a miracle. It should just happen. I knew as soon as I saw you that you were going to be important to me. I tried to think I was wrong, but I can't fight it."

"Neither can I."

"It's against all reason ... and yet it makes perfect sense. Say you feel that, too."

"Yes ... yes ..."

"I know now why you teased me in the gym the other day," he said with a chuckle. "You knew I was resisting you, and you weren't going to let me."

"I don't ever want you to be able to resist me," she said passionately.

"You were right. Some things shouldn't be resisted. Faye, let's get out of here. I can't hold you the way I want to in this place."

They returned to the table and gathered their things. Jason paid the bill, then took her hand and they hurried outside. The night air was soft and warm, and the stars above them were brilliant. They went through the parking lot to where they could find privacy in a small clump of trees, and there Jason pulled her urgently into his arms. Faye gave herself eagerly to his questing lips and found that the feel of his firm mouth on hers was a thousand times sweeter than she'd remembered. He kissed her hungrily, like a man who couldn't believe a beautiful dream and wanted to revel in it before it was snatched away.

For a brief moment Jason was amazed at himself. What had become of the caution he'd sworn to observe in all his dealings? But he knew this was no time for caution. She overwhelmed him with her loveliness, her warmth and a kind of trusting eagerness that touched his heart. She was good; every instinct told him that. Her beauty went deep down to her soul, making a nonsense of her tinsel trappings. He knew he must explore this paradox soon, but for now it was enough to hold her in his arms, rejoicing in the promise of her trembling body.

"Faye...Faye...." he couldn't say anything else, only her name in wonder.

"Hold me," she murmured against his mouth.

"I want to hold you...always. I want everything with you."

"Yes," she whispered.

"Come home with me now." He loosened his hold on her as he spoke, waiting for her answer. She stepped back and held out her hand in invitation. Mutely he put his own hand in hers and let her lead him to the car. He would have followed her anywhere.

Once inside the car the shadows enclosed them and instead of starting the engine he drew her to him again, kissing her hungrily, silently asking for reassurance that this was real. With every caress she made him a thousand promises. Happiness seized him and he dropped his head to let his lips rest against the hollow of her throat and she moved in his arms as though electricity had gone through her.

Faye hadn't known that her neck was so exquisitely sensitive until he rested his mouth against it and fire forked through her. As he kissed her throat once more she moaned and Jason began to slide his fingertips gently around her neck until he could caress the nape. She arched against him, thrilled by the sensation, but almost at once she took hold of his hand and murmured a reluctant, "No, not here . . . Jason."

"You're right," he said, fighting to control himself. "We have to go home first."

As they drove, Jason glanced out the corner of his eye and saw that she was looking at him almost with bewilderment. He understood exactly how she felt. He'd known that he wanted her, but what had happened between them tonight was something else. It was too soon for love. He told himself that as though touching a protective talisman. But he knew it was more, much more, than desire. His heart was involved with her in a way that already scared him.

He slipped his arm around her shoulders, drawing her closer, and something caught in his throat as he heard her little sigh of bliss. "You know we're doing something illegal, don't you?" he murmured.

She brushed her cheek against his hand. "Feeling like this is illegal?"

"Driving with my arm around you is against the law. If I was still on the force I'd have to book myself."

She chuckled huskily, causing him to tighten his arm and bury his mouth in her sweet-smelling hair. The car swerved and he gave the road his reluctant attention. "How lucky that the road is quiet," he said, "otherwise I'm not sure we'd get home."

"And I want to get home," she said languorously.

"Yes, so do I."

They drove the rest of the way in silence, satiated by the happiness of being together and the thought of the passion to come. When at last the car drew up outside the house Jason took her face between his hands and searched it anxiously. "I haven't misunderstood, have I?" he asked.

"No, you haven't misunderstood, Jason. What you feel, I feel."

"Bless you for that," he said in a shaky voice.

He pushed open the front door very quietly, but not quietly enough to escape Buck, who had been dozing on a sofa in the hall. He was alert at once and hurried across to greet them, tail wagging. They petted him, silently sharing their joy with him. Then Jason said, "Feel this."

He guided Faye's hand through the thickness of fur on Buck's shoulder until she could feel a long, jagged scar. "Poor old boy," she said, giving Buck a special hug. "That must have been a terrible wound."

"It was," Jason agreed. "You see why I feel I owe him?"

"But you mustn't blame yourself. It wasn't your fault Wainright was a crook."

She knew at once that she'd said something wrong. Jason's eyes narrowed. "Wainright?" he echoed.

"Yes. Wasn't he the man who...?"

"Yes, it was Wainright, but how do you know that? I never mentioned his last name, and the cover-up was so good that it never reached the papers." When she didn't answer he repeated in a hard voice, "So how did you know his name, Faye?"

"Does it matter? Jason I—"

"Yes, it matters. There's no way you could have come out with that name unless—unless you already knew everything I told you tonight." As he said the words a look of incredulous realization came over his face. "You did, didn't you?"

"The outline, yes," she admitted unhappily.

"Niall must have told you." Anger added an edge to his voice. "What else did he say? That a crooked cop is the best kind of 'fighting machine' there is?"

This was uncomfortably close to the truth and she flinched. Seeing it, Jason's bitterness increased. "So the two of you put your heads together—"

"No, it wasn't like that," she protested, talking too fast to think. "He keeps everyone's details on a computer—"

Jason's mirthless laughter cracked the air. "My God, that's wonderful. Here I was pouring out the story of my life, confiding things so painful that I've never told them to another living soul, even thinking

I could fall in love with you because your warmth seemed to reach out and touch me. And you'd read it all first *on a computer*. I could die laughing at that."

"Jason listen to me, *please*. Conroy keeps everyone on computer. Even me, probably—"

"You? Of course he has a file on you. You're a precious investment. You'll be the ideal wife for him, Faye: cold, calculating and manipulative. My God, you played your part well tonight. That sweet, sympathetic woman I thought I could love was actually no more than 'the boss lady' passing the time. I'm glad I entertained you well."

"Don't talk like that. Let me explain."

"Oh, no. None of your explanations. I've learned my lesson. Perhaps you'll be good enough to stay here while I fix your windows. Good night, Mrs. Niall."

He walked away without looking back. Instead of following him Buck looked anxiously at Faye as if hoping she would do something to ease the hostility he'd sensed. Halfway up the stairs Jason turned. "Buck," he called curtly.

The dog nuzzled Faye briefly, then turned and followed his master.

Faye gazed after Jason, bitterly blaming herself. She'd tricked him into going out with her, but after that her behavior had been utterly sincere. She'd thought only of him and the beauty that was growing between them. Entranced by that magic she'd allowed herself to forget her other purpose, and had been caught off guard.

She tried to believe that the pain that shook her was because she'd made a clumsy move. But it didn't work. The disillusion in Jason's face had torn her heart, and she knew she would never forgive herself for hurting him.

The following day Alaric seemed tired and readily accepted her suggestion that he stay in bed. Faye remained with him, reading to him when he was awake and watching over him while he slept. To her frantic, loving eyes his face looked more haggard in sleep, and she realized that he, too, was putting on an act, pretending to be better than he was to save her from worry. Now she could see the truth, and the truth was a sick man, prematurely aged by fear.

Her mind went back to the days before Alaric had lost their capital, when he'd been able to live in his study, writing. He'd always been there when she came home from school and together they'd escaped into an enchanted land. It didn't matter to them that few others seemed to want his books. He'd solemnly presented her with copies of all his volumes, inscribed, "To Faye, with love from Daddy," and she'd done her best to read the unreadable prose, which was turgid and elaborate, different from his flowing, caustic speech. They'd been two against the world, and content to be so. Alaric might be vague and hopelessly unreliable, but he'd forged an unbreakable bond of love with his daughter, and she was fiercely determined to protect him now.

Once he stirred and began muttering in his sleep. Faye listened, her heart torn with pity, as he babbled, "...had to do it...not prison...please, Mr. Niall...not prison...please..." The tortured words revealed the depth of the nightmare that haunted him night and day. She kissed him and whispered, "It's all right. Everything's going to be fine."

He opened his eyes and she smiled quickly. "I thought I heard you saying everything would be fine," he murmured. "Did I dream that?"

"No, I really said it."

Their eyes met for a long moment, then, as if it was torn from him with great effort, Alaric said, "It *is* all right, isn't it? You are happy, aren't you, darling? Because if not—I wouldn't want you to marry Conroy if—if—"

His breath became labored. Terrified, Faye burst out, "You mustn't worry about me. I want to marry Conroy, truly I do."

"You're not in love with him," Alaric said wearily. "I know that."

She rejected the idea of trying to convince him otherwise. Alaric might be muddleheaded but in his own way he was shrewd. "No, I'm not," she conceded cautiously. "But being 'in love' isn't everything. I'm fond of Conroy, and it's time I settled down. My career is over, and now I want something else." She tried to make her voice light. "There are worse things in the world than being married to a multimillionaire who's crazy about me."

She wondered just what he'd allowed himself to recognize in his inner heart. Alaric knew Conroy could incriminate him. Yet somehow he'd persuaded himself that Faye's sudden engagement to a man she'd always disliked was coincidence. He believed it because he desperately needed to believe it, but occasionally the protective facade cracked. "You're telling me the truth?" he persisted, searching her face.

She put all the conviction she could manage into saying, "Honestly, Daddy, it's the truth."

He smiled. "You haven't called me Daddy for years."

"I was remembering when I was a little girl and we used to shut ourselves up in your study, and you told me wonderful stories about knights and ladies, dragons and sorcerers. Remember how we used to plan to visit that place that's supposed to be the original of Camelot?"

"I remember, darling," he said gently. "Perhaps we can still go."

She tried to say brightly, "Of course we will." But suddenly her courage wavered and she laid her head down on his shoulder. "Everything was so easy in those days, wasn't it, Daddy?" she whispered longingly.

He sighed. "Yes, darling, it was."

She felt his arm go around her, and lay there quietly thinking how much she loved him, and yet wishing that in all the world there was one person who would share her burdens.

As if in answer to the thought she heard Jason calling her name from the grounds. Her heart leaped with hope and she jumped up to go to the window. But her smile faded as she saw Jason standing there, the look on his face as cold and unyielding as ever. "I have some news that will make your day," he said ironically. "Your fiancé is paying you a surprise visit."

She paled. "When?"

"Right now. I just glimpsed his car coming up the driveway. Isn't that wonderful?"

"Just incredible," she said, matching his cold tone.

She turned back into the room. "Conroy's here," she told Alaric, sounding as cheerful as she could.

"Splendid, I was just about to get up."

"No, please..."

But Alaric flung back the covers and began to put on his dressing gown. To her relief Faye could see that his movements were more vigorous. At last he put his arm through hers and they went out to the front step, arriving just as Conroy's Rolls-Royce drew up.

She tried to make her mind a blank when Conroy flung an arm around her shoulder and drew her close for a crushing kiss, but she was burningly aware of Jason watching them with a derisive look on his face that most likely mirrored his thoughts. Beside him stood Buck, totally still except for the hairs that arose instinctively on his back at the sight of Conroy. "Sweetie," Conroy growled. "It's good to see you again. Let me look at you."

He held her at arm's length and surveyed her from head to toe. She endured his raking look, but the empathy that linked her heart to Jason even when they were at odds with each other made her see the action through his eyes: the speculator checking out the property to see if it was still worth what he was paying. She wished the ground could open and swallow her. "This is a wonderful surprise," she managed to say. "Why didn't you let me know you were coming?"

"It was an impulse," he grated. "I couldn't go another hour without seeing you. A man shouldn't be separated too long from his bride-to-be. It's bad for both of them."

"That's very true, darling," Alaric told her eagerly. "At least you won't have a neglectful husband."

"Faye's too beautiful to neglect," Conroy asserted, running a finger down her neck until it rested against the hollow of her throat. Faye resisted the impulse to throw it off. "And I can promise you that you need have no fears for your daughter. I'm always attentive, aren't I, darling?"

"Always," she managed to say brightly. "Will you be staying long?"

"I shall stay tonight, and maybe tomorrow night." His eyes were hot as they regarded her. "Let's see how things work out."

He released her and started up the steps. Faye stayed a moment to still her shuddering, then forced herself to look in Jason's direction. But he'd gone.

Conroy's first destination was Alaric's room, which he inspected in detail. "I made a point of telling them to put you on the ground floor so that you wouldn't have the strain of climbing stairs," he asserted. "And your nurse? How do you find him?"

"He's excellent," Alaric said. "I couldn't ask for better care."

"I insisted that the agency give me the best they had. I told them this was someone very important to me."

Faye turned away so that Conroy wouldn't see the cynical look on her face. Of course Alaric was important to him. Without her father he had no hold over her.

Conroy continued inspecting the room, commenting with loud approval on the pleasant view, the specially bought bed that was neither to high nor too low, the discreetly stored oxygen equipment in case of another attack. An observer might have seen in him a kindly, concerned man, anxious to please his future wife. But Faye knew he was reminding her of all the ways in which Alaric depended on him.

Conroy took in the sight of Alaric's dressing gown. "I hope you haven't taken a turn for the worst," he said.

"No, just resting," Alaric assured him. "But I'll be up for the meal tonight."

"Fine. I'll look forward to seeing you then."

Conroy put his arm around Faye's waist and drew her from the room. As soon as they were out of earshot he demanded, "Why are you dressed like that?"

"What's wrong with the way I'm dressed?" she said, freeing herself and looking down at her casual shirt and jeans.

"Everything. I never gave you those rags."

"This is the country, Conroy. People dress casually."

"You can dress decently even in the country. I've given you good clothes and I expect you to wear them. I want you properly dressed for dinner tonight."

"What does that mean?"

"It means the full works. Wear that black evening gown."

She sighed. The gown was a lavish creation of black satin, heavily embroidered with silver thread, that left her shoulders completely bare. Faye hated it, and was convinced that the designer had produced it only because he'd recognized that Conroy was a man who would buy anything if it cost enough. "That dress would be too much at a banquet," she said firmly. "For you, me and Dad it's ridiculous."

"It's what I want," Conroy said in a voice of finality. "By the way, Royce will be dining with us, too."

"He doesn't usually eat with us."

"Why not? Are you giving him a hard time? I told you not to. He's carrying out my orders."

"I'm not giving him a hard time—"

"Come to think of it, I thought I noticed a certain chill between you two."

"You can't have noticed anything. You only saw us together for a moment."

"These things have a way of being obvious." He smiled nastily. "And I remember just how haughty you can be when you take a dislike to a man."

Faye shrugged, glad at least that Conroy was too emotionally stupid to detect the real current that ran between her and Jason. She tried to move away up the stairs but Conroy followed her, still talking. "I want no looking down your nose. You're to be nice to him."

Faye stopped abruptly and wheeled around, eyes flashing with scorn. "You'd better define 'nice,' Conroy. Do you mean 'nice' as I had to be to that greasy banker, or real first-degree 'niceness' like you wanted me to show to poor little Mr. Freeman, whom you were trying to ruin?"

"But I didn't succeed. Freeman managed to get a bridging loan the very morning I was due to move against him. Someone tipped him off. You wouldn't know who, would you, Faye?"

"Go to hell," she said softly.

He grinned, pleased at having made her angry. "I leave the details to you, sweetheart, but remember Royce is a man I'm thinking of taking into my organization, and I don't want him antagonized."

"You can get a bodyguard anywhere," she snapped to cover her dismay.

"He may be a bodyguard now, but I plan bigger and better things for him. He's intelligent, which makes a nice change from the usual goons working for me. I could even groom him to become my second in command, which means he'll be spending a lot of time with us. So you'd better learn to get used to him."

Faye's heart almost failed her at the thought of having Jason constantly around, and if she couldn't save herself, the witness to her dreadful marriage. But she managed to laugh derisively and say, "You're wasting your time. He wouldn't be interested. For one thing, Buck doesn't like you."

"Who the hell is Buck and why should I worry what he thinks?"

"Buck is Jason's dog and he loathed you on sight. Look at his fangs sometime, Conroy. They're enormous, and he'd like nothing better than to have you for breakfast."

Conroy laughed. "Now I've heard everything. You think any man will turn down the chance of a lifetime for a dog? You've misread Jason Royce. Fundamentally he's like me."

"Never." The word escaped before she could stop it.

"You think not? Know what he told me once? That he likes my kind of corruption because it's *honest* corruption. It doesn't pretend to be anything else. I can deal with a man who thinks like that. He has the makings of a magnificent—shall we say, 'entrepreneur'?"

"No, let's say crook," Faye snapped. "It's what you mean."

"Whatever you choose to call it," Conroy conceded with a shrug. "He gave his allegiance to the wrong people, now he gives it to me. He's *my* man, body and soul, and more useful to me than all the others put together. I'm telling you this so that you understand the situation and do your duty. Royce will eat with us tonight. And we'd better have Don as well, just in case your father gets close to expiring from delight."

"My God, you are loathsome," Faye snapped, driven beyond endurance by his callous mention of Alaric's weakness.

"We'll make a little party of it," Conroy continued, indifferent to her anger. "You and I never had a proper engagement party because of Alaric's health. But now he's better we can celebrate a little."

"I don't want to," she said firmly.

"I didn't ask what you wanted. I'm telling you what you'll do. I want you in that perfume I bought you. It cost two hundred pounds for a thimbleful, but I know you never wear it unless I insist."

"Did you ever wonder why?" she asked sarcastically.

"I don't give a damn why. *Wear it.* And wear the black dress, like I told you." His eyes narrowed. "You did bring it, didn't you?"

"Yes, I obeyed your instructions. But I hate that dress. It's vulgar."

"Vulgar? It cost me five thousand pounds. How can it be vulgar? Now look, Faye, there's got to be an end to this nonsense. You'll do as I say and you'll dress as I say. If I tell you to smile, you'll smile, and when I want you to look pleased you'll look pleased. Do you understand?" When she tried to turn away without answering he stopped her with a hard grip on her arm. *"Do you understand?"*

Faye regarded him bleakly. "If you bruise my arm it'll spoil the illusion you're trying to create."

He loosened his grip and she wrenched herself free, running the rest of the way upstairs until she reached her room and could put a door between them. She'd won a small battle by refusing to give him the docile answer he'd wanted, but Conroy was winning the war because he had all the weapons. Jason had been her only hope, and she'd alienated him.

She tried not to look at the hideous picture Conroy had held up to her: Jason, second in command in a crooked empire, using all his strength and skill in the service of evil as he'd once used it for good, and always around to torture her with the memory of passion that had almost been fulfilled.

In her worst nightmares Faye had never thought of anything so horrible. Her heart told her that the man she was beginning to love was too fine to stoop to baseness, but what did she really know about Jason? The man he'd admired and loved as a father had betrayed him. Now his view of the world was distorted, and she herself had accidentally reinforced his cynicism. He knew what his employer was, yet he was working for him. What was to stop him from betraying her to Conroy?

At last she reluctantly started to get ready for the evening. She'd brought the black gown on Conroy's orders, but the thought of wearing it revolted her. The neckline plunged and the tight waist emphasized the swell of her high, firm breasts. Both it and the perfume were blatantly glamorous, the trappings of a woman who wanted men to lust after her. Faye shuddered as she thought of Conroy gloating as he displayed his possession, and the derision she would see in Jason's eyes.

She delayed joining them as long as possible, but at last she could find no further excuses. She took a deep breath and went downstairs to an evening she knew was going to be an ordeal.

Chapter Seven

Faye found the men already gathered, sipping drinks. Conroy had carried out his threat to make the evening a formal party and was attired in a dinner jacket. Jason wore the same, presumably on his employer's orders. Don and Alaric were dressed in ordinary clothes. "I thought you were never coming, darling," Conroy said.

"I took extra time and trouble," she said mechanically.

"How sweet of you. Gentlemen, allow me to present my bride, the future Mrs. Conroy Niall."

The other three murmured appropriate noises and Alaric raised his glass to Faye. She was glad to notice that he seemed lively and cheerful this evening.

"A drink, darling?" Conroy asked.

"I'd like a dry sherry, please."

Jason fetched it, managing to hand it to her without letting their fingers touch. Conroy had turned away to speak to Alaric. "I don't see Buck tonight," she remarked to Jason.

"He preferred to stay in the kitchen." Jason's cold eyes met hers as he added, "He doesn't like the company."

Faye's temper rose. "How dare you!" she said softly. "What right do you have to judge me?"

After a moment he looked away. "None," he said.

"We're having a celebration tonight," Conroy declared. "First we're celebrating the recovery of my future father-in-law. And second we're celebrating my engagement to the most beautiful woman in the world."

He lifted her hand to his lips. Faye was still angry with Jason, and now she was glad of it. It sustained her and enabled her to give Conroy a glittering smile. "You shouldn't pay me extravagant compliments in public, darling," she said. "You're embarrassing me."

"I guess you'll just have to get used to being told how beautiful you are," he responded. "And it's my pleasure to make you even more beautiful. I brought your engagement present with me."

"I wasn't expecting another gift when you've given me so much . . ."

"I know you weren't. That's where the fun comes in. Here you are." He flourished a black box in front of her. "Open it." She did so and was almost blinded by the flash of diamonds within. A heavy necklace lay against black velvet, blazing with white fire. "For the future Mrs. Niall," Conroy declared. "It'll do you more justice than that skimpy thing you're wearing." Faye had put on the delicate pendant that she'd worn the night before. Now Conroy indicated it, saying, "Take it off."

She felt for the clasp behind her neck, but it kept slipping from her fingers. Conroy had taken the necklace from the box and stood holding it impatiently. Then Jason moved quietly behind her and opened the clasp. His fingers brushed against her nape and for a moment Faye almost lost control as memories of the night before came surging back. She could feel his breath against her skin and it was fiery hot, as hot as it had been when he'd held her in his arms and spoken her name over and over.

Then his touch was gone. He took a step away from her and held out the pendant for her to take. His manner was calm and composed, but his hands were shaking.

For Jason it had been an ordeal to step close to her. He didn't want to breathe in the sultry, languorous perfume that arose from her warm flesh. It was a wanton scent that hinted at passion and invitation—at a price. It was unlike anything he'd ever smelled on her before, and her wearing it for Conroy Niall told its own story.

There were other signs, too. Jason would have fiercely denied that there was anything fanciful in his nature, yet he couldn't help seeing something symbolic in the removal of the delicate pendant from Faye's neck, and her assumption of the diamond halter. It said more clearly than words that she'd made her choice.

He tried not to look as Conroy draped a fortune around her throat but he was sharply aware of the other man's fingers against her soft skin. Pain gnawed at him as he recalled how he had touched her there, kissing her until she moaned with delight. And now she stood smiling at Conroy, calling him "darling." Jason made his way unobtrusively to the drinks cabinet, exchanged his glass of Perrier water for a brandy and downed it with one gulp.

She looked like a queen, he thought, as she swept into the dining room on Conroy's arm. Her head had an arrogant tilt. She'd asked what right he had to judge her. He'd said "None," but it wasn't true. He had every right because of what she'd done to him, because of what she was doing this minute. As they seated themselves at the table he found he was directly opposite her. Behind him was another liquor cabinet and he quietly poured some more brandy into his empty glass. Normally he never touched alcohol, but tonight he was going to need help.

He became aware that Alaric was saying something to him and answered mechanically. He didn't know what he'd said. His gaze was fixed on Faye as she sat beside Conroy, beautiful, aloof, looking mysteriously untouched and untouchable. But then, unnervingly, his perspective shifted, and again he felt the way he had in the gym, that she was another woman, one who radiated a feverish eroticism, a blatant lust for life and love that was at variance with Faye's delicate sensuality. It was the strange perfume, he told himself. And then the moment passed, leaving only the faint reverberations of an echo.

He knew he shouldn't torment himself, but he couldn't tear his eyes away. Her skin glowed softly, tempting him to lay his lips against it, but Conroy's gaudy badge of ownership lay between them. If she'd been his he would have bought her not diamonds but pearls whose soft radiance would have set off her own.

Then he remembered that he couldn't afford the kind of luxury that this woman took for granted. But there were always fake pearls. He would buy her jewels that were as fake as she was herself. Look how she gazed at her tainted prize, he thought, letting Niall hold her hand between his two ugly ones, not flinching as he gazed at her revealing neckline. Jason drained his glass again and felt for the bottle.

At last it started to happen, the thing he'd been praying for, a warmth that spread upward from the pit of his stomach, engulfing him in a protective cocoon. Now the pain seemed to reach him through a layer of cotton wool, and he could listen dispassionately to Conroy saying, "I don't know if Faye ever told you about our romance..."

He could even reply cheerfully, "No, she never did."

"It was all very sudden, wasn't it, darling?"

"Totally unexpected," she agreed.

"What you might call a whirlwind courtship. But I don't believe in wasting time. When I realized I had a chance with this beautiful woman I said what I had to say while I had the courage, and to my surprise she turned out to feel the same. I guess you never know what lucky breaks life has in store for you."

"Conroy," she protested. "I'm sure Jason and Don aren't interested—"

"But of course they are," Conroy interrupted her. "All the world loves a lover. And tonight I want to concentrate on you. Do you know how many deals I've left hanging in the fire to come down here to see you?"

"Now I *know* you're devoted to me," she murmured ironically.

"When I make a decision it's final, and the decision I made was to come here and set our wedding date and get you to decide where you want to go for our honeymoon."

"Conroy," she began desperately, "I don't think..."

"How about somewhere exotic? You'd like that, wouldn't you? I've heard that Hong Kong is quite a place."

And you have quite a few irons in the fire in Hong Kong, Jason thought cynically. *Never waste an opportunity to give them a stir.*

"I really don't mind where we go," Faye said.

"Hong Kong then?" Conroy persisted.

"All right. Hong Kong."

"So my bride wants to go to Hong Kong and as I'll do whatever she asks—Hong Kong it is. All that's left is to set the date—"

"Which we can't do until the doctor gives Dad another checkup," Faye broke in, feeling she would go mad if this conversation didn't end soon. She managed to catch Conroy's eye, sending him a silent message to stop this. His cold face seemed to jeer back at her, but it was he who wavered first, and he didn't mention the date again.

"You'd better pour me a brandy," Conroy said, thrusting his glass in Jason's direction.

Jason examined the brandy decanter and to his surprise found it empty. Faye quietly summoned Martha to bring some more and Conroy said with heavy jocularity, "It's not like you to knock it back, Jason. Does the subject matter depress you? Are you a married man?"

You know I'm not, Jason thought. *It's all on your computer. And that tense look on your fiancée's face is because she's worried how much I'm going to say about last night. How easy it is to read her now that I know she's fake all the way through.*

"No, I'm not married," he replied.

"Spoken for?"

"No, nor ever likely to be."

"No female entanglements? Wise man."

Jason surveyed his employer with careful gravity. "So you don't think that all men should seek the same happiness you've found?" he queried.

"Only if they can get a woman like Faye," Conroy replied. "And there are no others like her."

"How true," Jason mused. "Your advice is excellent. I don't mean to get tied up until I can find a female who'll stick by me as faithfully as my dog."

Conroy broke out with coarse laughter. Alaric and Don smiled nervously, uncertain how to take the conversation. Faye looked at Jason with defiant eyes. "Perhaps a dog is all you're capable of loving," she said, and had the satisfaction of knowing she'd taken him aback.

"You talk like a man who's had a bitter experience," Conroy observed.

"Bitter but not wasted," Jason assured him.

"Tell us about it," Conroy demanded with an air of enjoyment.

"It's the oldest story in the book," Jason said with a shrug. "The woman was diabolically clever, the man was a naive fool." He poured himself another glass and added reflectively, "What made him an even bigger fool was his conviction—which seems laughable in retrospect—that he was clear-sighted enough to see through the subtlest female schemes. Of course that made him putty in her hands. He had no one but himself to blame for what happened."

"So you were taken for a sucker?" Conroy asked, grinning.

"Taken good," Jason confirmed and drained his glass.

"What do you think of that, darling?" Conroy demanded of Faye.

"I think," Faye said slowly and with deliberate emphasis, "that I've never heard such a load of self-pitying rubbish spoken by a man who didn't have the faintest idea what he was talking about. You know nothing about women or how their minds work, Jason. Take that from a woman. I think you should stop and wonder about *her* opinion of *your* behavior. She might say something uncomfortable about men who make glib, superficial judgments."

Jason recovered from her surprise counterattack sufficiently enough to say, "Perhaps she would. But you see I never really knew what was in her mind." He felt an unwilling increase of respect for her.

"I think the time has come for a little toast," Conroy declared, rising to his feet. "Gentlemen, I give you the future Mrs. Niall."

Somewhere Jason found the strength to get to his feet and stand there steadily while he raised his glass to Faye. "The future Mrs. Niall," he said. "And now, if you'll excuse me, it's getting late and I have duties to perform."

Years of tough training helped him walk impassively to the door, open it and close it behind him without looking back at her. Then he left the house as if all the furies of hell were pursuing him.

The stars overhead were brilliant and cold. Once outside Jason stood inhaling the fresh night air, trying to clear his head. It wasn't easy because half of him didn't want to see the world clearly ever again, but gradually the edges became sharp.

Buck, who'd been dozing in the hall, had awakened instantly and followed him out. They patrolled the grounds together, taking it slowly because Jason was determined to stay outside until the others had gone to bed. When he'd finished his rounds he stood, one hand absently caressing Buck's head, and noted when the lights began to change. Some of the downstairs rooms plunged into darkness, then a light came on in Faye's room. At last he began to trudge reluctantly back toward the building, with Buck walking quietly at his heels.

They went in through the back door, and made their way across the darkened hall. There was a thin strip of light under Alaric's door and Jason could hear Don moving around inside. He went up the main staircase, Buck slightly ahead, and then nearly stumbled as the dog froze. Jason touched him and felt the hairs rising on his back. Then he understood why.

On the landing just ahead of them stood Conroy Niall, dressed in pajamas and a robe. He was standing by a window, smoking a cigar and staring out. Jason stayed motionless, watching him, hearing his own heart beat with an apprehension he wouldn't acknowledge. If Niall had just left his own room he was headed for the corridor that housed Faye and Jason himself. For a wild moment he indulged the hope that his employer would knock on his door wanting to talk about security.

But then Niall stubbed out the cigar and continued his journey. He passed Jason's door without a pause and vanished from sight. Jason listened with painful intensity and heard a faint knock, then the sound of a door being opened and closed again. When he moved quietly up to the corridor there was no sign of Niall, and as he stared at Faye's door he heard a bolt shoot home on the other side.

So what the hell? He'd known about her and there was nothing about this that should shock or even surprise him.

But it *was* a shock. It was a hammer blow in the guts, winding him and making his head spin. He steadied himself against the wall, taking deep breaths until he could move again. Then he slipped down the stairs and back outside and gulped in the cool air, trying to ease the feeling of choking.

Faye and Niall together! He'd thought he'd known torment throughout the evening, but it had been nothing compared to this. That mean, ferret-faced little bully had the right to take her in his arms as he, Jason, had done, and feel her slim, young body against his own. He'd paid for that right in hard cash, and the woman who'd calculated the odds before she accepted his ring would know how to give full value in exchange. Jason was trembling.

He ran until he reached the lake, stripped naked and plunged into the chilly water, seeking balm for the fever that consumed him. But the misery was still there: Faye and Niall, locked in the union that should symbolize love, debasing it to the level of a banking transaction. The thought battered him until he wanted to commit violence to escape it.

He circled below the water for as long as he had breath, then surfaced. There was a slight noise on the bank and he realized Buck was there, keeping away, as though not wanting to intrude. The dog had settled down by the water's edge to wait for his master.

He could see the turret that he knew was Faye's. Conroy stood in one of the windows, silhouetted against the light. Suddenly his arm went around Faye, pulling her close, and he bent his head to kiss the base of her throat. After what seemed like an age Faye's arm went up around his neck and she began to kiss him back.

Jason stayed as he was, listening to the sound of his own heart thundering against his ribs. Then he drew in his breath sharply as Conroy lifted Faye in his arms and turned away to carry her into the room. He stared at the empty place in the window for a long, desperate moment, before plunging back into the lake, swimming hard for its full length. The water was chilly against his skin but he was burning nonetheless. At the far side he twisted and swam back underwater for as long as he could. He surfaced gasping and swam on with vigorous strokes, refusing to look up.

When he returned Buck was still waiting for him, as motionless as a sphinx. Now Jason looked at the house, and a deep groan broke from him as he saw that the light in Faye's room had gone out. He closed his eyes and dropped his head against the dog's fur. He buried his face deep in it, pressing tightly, but nothing could blot out the monstrous picture in his mind of Faye and Niall—together.

Conroy closed the door of Faye's bedroom behind him and shot the bolt home. "Now we won't be disturbed," he said.

Faye didn't answer and he stood watching her, smiling a small secret smile. He enjoyed the restless way she paced the room, and the trapped look in her eyes as she saw him standing between her and the door. The only thing that didn't please him was the fact that she was still fully dressed. "I had hoped to find you wearing something a little more welcoming," he said.

"What were you expecting—negligee, peignoir and seductive scent?" she flashed. "You know better than that, Conroy—or you ought to."

"I know I'm entitled to a damn sight more than I'm getting from you. Don't you think it's time you loosened up a bit, my dear?" He touched the diamonds, which she'd tossed indifferently onto the dressing table. "You can't say I'm not generous. These cost me a pretty penny."

"I've already gone through the motions of undying gratitude," she snapped.

"Yes, you accepted them very prettily. Your father was so pleased to see you happy with me. What a pity that he has to be there before you show me any warmth."

"If it wasn't for my father I'd never agree to be in the same room with you," she said coldly.

"Yes, I know. It's really rather forbearing of me not to retaliate for your unkindness, don't you think?"

"I'm sure you have every intention of retaliating just as soon as my prison door has clanged shut," Faye retorted.

Conroy laughed silently in a way that made her blood run cold. "How well you're beginning to know me, my fairy Faye. You're quite right, of course. Having you is going to be a banquet that I want to savor at leisure. I can wait. After all, our wedding day is very near now."

Faye regarded him with hate-filled eyes. Conroy went to stand by the window. "I thought your father was in particularly good form tonight," he remarked. "Splendid considering how recently he was at death's door. I gather you've managed to keep him ignorant of quite a few things."

"He doesn't know that our engagement was the price of his freedom," Faye said tersely.

Conroy looked at her swiftly, his eyes hard. "Oh, no, my lovely. It's our marriage that will be the price of his freedom, and don't you ever forget that. I still have papers that prove he's a thief." He reached out suddenly and pulled her tightly against him. "You were very silly thinking I'd hand them over at our engagement party."

She fought to control her nausea at his nearness. "You promised me that you would," she managed to say.

He dropped his head to kiss the base of her throat. "Well, you should have known better than to believe my word, shouldn't you?" he murmured. "I didn't believe *your* word when you said you'd marry me after I'd given up the evidence. Of course you wouldn't. But you'll marry me while I'm still holding it, because otherwise he'll go to jail and that would finish him. No, don't jerk away darling. Your skin is so soft and smooth just here—and here—" His lips were drifting lower.

Faye tried to shut off her mind and deaden sensation so that she wouldn't feel his burning breath. But it was useless. With every hated touch her disgust grew until she felt weak. She knew Conroy was relishing his power. He wouldn't be interested in love even if she had it to give. For him the joy of life was domination, and the domination of an unwilling woman was the greatest thrill of all.

Tonight it was worse because now she had the memory of being held in Jason's arms, her lips burned by his kisses, her body melted by the fire of his ardor. The very thought of him could inflame her with passionate longing, making this assault from a man she loathed even more unendurable. But it was vital that Conroy be lulled into a false sense of security, so she swallowed her feelings and tried to think of Jason as she forced her arms upward about Conroy's neck.

He laughed down into her face. "So you're learning which side your bread is buttered on at last. I like a woman with brains enough to treat me right. Kiss me. Kiss me as if you mean it."

She made herself comply, and felt him lift her into his arms and turn away from the window to carry her to the bed. But as he laid her on it she wrenched away. *"No,"* she said violently. "Not yet."

"I'm in the mood now," he grated. "If you aren't willing, I might go downstairs and have a word with your father about his future."

"You won't do that," she said, trying to sound confident, "because if you did you'd never get what you want. That would be a pity after you've worked so hard for it."

He grinned, a nasty, vile stretching of his mouth. "I'm going to enjoy being married to you, sweetie. I'm going to enjoy it very much."

"But we aren't married yet. I want you to leave my room, Conroy."

"You're really something, you know that? You couldn't do a damn thing if I refuse."

"Go *now*."

Suddenly he seemed to lose interest in his cat-and-mouse game, and got up from the bed. "Just don't forget that you're my property," he warned. "Bought and paid for, and very soon I want you delivered. Set the wedding date quickly. Or else!" He pulled back the bolt on the door and strode out without a backward glance.

Faye instantly leaped up and ran to the door. She thrust the bolt home with all her strength, then fled into her bathroom. She wrenched off her clothes and got under the shower, scrubbing herself down repeatedly, wondering how she would ever feel clean again. When she'd finished she leaned against the wall, gasping, her wet hair plastered to her neck and shoulders.

At last she stepped out of the shower, toweled herself dry and slipped on her negligee. Then she turned out all the lights, went to the open window and stood there in the darkness, enjoying the peace. Above her head the clear, cold stars sparkled in their eternal orbit, indifferent to her grief.

Then she froze as a soft moaning sound, like a soul in torment, floated up on the night air. She tensed, listening. But there was only silence, and at last she realized that the sound must have been the wind sighing in the trees.

Chapter Eight

Faye's legs ached but she forced herself to sink into the plié, feeling her thigh muscles protest as she rose again. Now down and up once more, turn on the bar, five pliés facing the other direction, feet in the fifth position and repeat the whole process before she could allow herself a rest. She was determined to stay at the bar for an hour and a half, as she'd once done every day when she was with the Kramer Ballet. Now her whole body was screaming but she refused to stop until she'd reached her target.

Conroy had departed early that morning and she'd escaped to the top of the house to immerse herself in dancing. There seemed to be no chance of her ever returning to her career, but she could find some peace by driving herself to the limit.

She finished the pliés, and stood for a moment, gasping slightly, gripping the bar against the giddiness that swept through her. She was wearing a pair of old black tights and a skimpy pink shirt, mended in several places. It was fixed in the front not by buttons, but by ends that tied. The knot kept coming loose and she tightened it again, then turned inward and raised her left leg until the heel could rest on the bar. With her left arm curved above her head she leaned forward and sideways until her forehead touched her knee, straightened up, leaned way back, holding the bar with her right hand, then forward again. The blood was pounding in her head. She closed her eyes, gritted her teeth and continued bending and stretching, lost in a world where there was only pain and determination.

She didn't hear Jason open the door of the gymnasium and enter quietly. He stood watching her, frowning. The black tights outlined her slim thighs and hips and for the first time he fully understood both the beauty and the delicate power of her compact frame. There wasn't an ounce of spare flesh on her. She looked as if a breath would blow her away. Yet as he observed the endless bending and stretching without a pause for breath, Jason, a trained athlete, was amazed to recognize her steely physical strength and the unyielding will that drove her spirit. The respect he'd felt for her last night revived, and to it was added a layer of pure professional admiration.

He moved forward to see her face. It was the first time he'd studied her closely without makeup and he realized how genuinely beautiful she was. For once the glorious golden hair wasn't tumbling around her shoulders. Pulled severely back into a net, it revealed the classic lines of her face—the high cheekbones and pointed jaw, and her long, elegant neck.

She was far too pale, there were dark smudges beneath her eyes and two faint lines had appeared on her forehead, the only outward sign of her ferocious inner concentration. But none of this detracted from her loveliness.

He had an impulse to reach forward and smooth the lines away, but he mastered it, knowing she wouldn't be pleased with his intrusion. She had withdrawn into another world where he didn't exist. It was yet one more piece in the puzzle that she constantly presented. Why should a woman who had schemed so successfully to enjoy a life of ease drive herself to the point of exhaustion, as though she were trying to exorcise some demon from her soul?

He thought of what he'd seen the night before and tried to remember that he hated her. But that was someone else, an artificial, bejeweled creature. *This* was the real Faye, this tense, vulnerable young woman who dipped and swayed so gracefully to her inner music.

Suddenly she stopped. She was leaning back, one hand still holding the bar, the other curved over her head. Jason saw her fight for the strength to raise herself upright, but the strength was no longer there and gradually her fingers released the bar. He leaped forward and caught her just before she slipped to the floor.

Faye's eyes flew open and she found herself looking up into Jason's face, his arms enclosing her. She couldn't think how he'd got there, unless he'd come out of her dream, but somehow she wasn't surprised.

Jason dropped to his knees and stayed motionless for a moment, holding Faye half lying, half sitting. He knew that he should let her go now, at once, but he couldn't make himself do it. It had already been too late the moment he touched her. The memory of their last embrace seemed to hang between them, making inevitable the moment when he dropped his head to brush his mouth against hers in a kiss they both longed for.

In the circle of Jason's arms Faye felt her weary body come to new life. All pain was forgotten in the magic sensation of being held close to him, of having his mouth explore hers. Until now they'd shared only a few kisses but already she knew his mouth, the enticing way it could move, tormenting her with promise. The touch of his tongue flickering against her lips brought a storm of glorious sensation.

She was wild with wanting him and the fierceness of that want shook her through and through. The hard tension that had gripped her during the misery of the past days melted and dissolved in the heat of his urgency, and her own that rose in response. Every inch of her flesh was soft now, as though it had been made for this moment of yielding. She parted her lips and rejoiced as he entered eagerly, seeking her with urgent forays of his tongue, caressing the soft inner flesh with the tip. She responded by arching against him, running her hands through his thick, dark hair, moaning softly in the depths of her throat.

"Faye...Faye..." He groaned her name again and again, and his voice held all his need and confusion, his passion for her and his distrust of her.

Faye could feel the pounding of his heart close to hers and she opened the buttons of his shirt so that she could run her hand over his chest. His muscles were hard against her palm and she seemed to vibrate with the same trembling that possessed him. "Dear God," he whispered desperately. "Why can't I stop myself from coming back to you?"

She slid her hand up until it touched his face, and drew it caressingly down near his jaw. "Because you *must* come to me," she murmured. "Because if you didn't, I'd come to you. I need you Jason...want you..." She was almost delirious with joy, barely knowing what she said. He didn't reply in words but she didn't care. The look in his eyes was enough.

"Can you forgive me, Faye?" he asked softly.

"There's nothing for me to forgive."

"But there is," he said. "If you knew how I hated you, how I *wanted* to hate you... You were right last night about superficial judgments. I was afraid I'd imagined what was between us," he said. "Afraid of *you*."

"How could you be afraid of me?" she asked wonderingly.

"Because suspicion is my curse," he groaned. "I believed anything but the truth, which is that we came together because we had to. I know there are still a thousand unanswered questions but right now I don't care. I know you. I know there's something good and true in you that can never be corrupted. Right this minute that's all I need to know."

As she heard his words, so full of trust, Faye felt a kind of horror. What would happen to Jason when she had to tell him the truth, that their relationship was founded on a deception? Could he possibly love her enough to understand?

While she was fretting about that thought he pulled the knot of her blouse until it fell open, revealing her naked breasts. He covered one with his hand and she drew in a shuddering breath at the pleasure that was a hundred times more sweet than she could have imagined. When he took a nipple teasingly between his finger and thumb she gasped. The tantalizing movements of his fingers sent waves of delight through her.

But it couldn't last. Her joy was poisoned by the guilt he'd unknowingly triggered in her. Her conscience seemed to claw her back from the brink of supreme joy, reminding her that she'd set out determinedly to win Jason over, without analyzing precisely what the expression meant. But it meant this. It meant seeing him gaze down on her with eyes that were hazy with desire, hearing him speak her name in a voice that trembled and knowing that he was as open and vulnerable to her as a boy.

"Faye..." Jason murmured against her lips. "Let me love you..."

"No..." She began to struggle. "Please, Jason. No."

"But you want me, I know you do..."

"Yes..." Her heart couldn't deny it. "Yes..."

She felt Jason's fingers move once more against her breast, caressing it skillfully, as though enticing her with the promise of delight to come. Fire streaked through her until she was dizzy with passion. Her whole body throbbed with the knowledge that this was the one man who could bring her fulfillment. It cost all her strength to push him away, but she knew she must. The time wasn't right.

As he felt her resist him determinedly Jason frowned. "Don't play games with me, Faye," he said. "You know what there is between us. What is it you want from me?"

"Just a little patience...." she managed to gasp.

"We're past that point. We're a man and a woman who want each other deeply. You can't deny it."

He pulled her to him again in a kiss of such sensual power that Faye felt her self-control slipping away. Terrified, she pushed him back then leaped nimbly to her feet and hastily clutched together the gaping edges of her shirt. She was burning with shame, and for a terrible moment shame was stronger than passion. Jason, too, had risen to his feet. He made a quick angry movement toward her and she threw up her head and faced him defiantly.

The gesture stopped Jason in his tracks. He stood quite still, staring at her, while recognition and anger dawned in his eyes. "Now I know where I've seen you before," he breathed. "You're Carmen."

He took a step back as if trying to break a spell and spoke half to himself. "Carmen—the Kramer Ballet. I saw a performance. It was you. I didn't recognize you without the black wig but just now, when you threw your head up—you made that same gesture in the last scene when Don José came crawling back to you, begging you to love him. It was you, wasn't it?"

"I danced Carmen with the Kramer Ballet, yes," she said. "But it was a role, that's all."

Jason grinned mirthlessly. "I wonder. You were far too convincing, Faye. Carmen was a woman who devoured men for pleasure. José never had a chance after you got your claws into him. Afterward he was just a husk. So I was right about you, after all! My God, to think I fell for it twice! You've been amusing yourself. A nice little flirtation; harmless enough as long as you don't go too far and lose Conroy Niall's millions. Then toss away the husk. He's just an employee.

"But I'm also a man, and I have too much pride to let that happen. Yes, I want you. I've never wanted a woman so much. Last night I went half crazy because he was in your bed—"

"He wasn't—"

"I thought that cured me of you, but today I only had to touch you to start shaking again. And that's what you like, isn't it? Get a man so besotted that he'll accept anything, even sharing you with another man. But not me. I won't pay your price."

He strode to the door but stopped at the sound of Faye calling his name. He looked back. She seemed to be having difficulty finding the words. At last she said, "Conroy wasn't in my bed last night."

"He was in your room," Jason snapped.

"Not for very long. I threw him out."

"Why should I believe you?"

She gave a wry laugh. "That's right. Why should you?"

He walked out.

He didn't join them for lunch, and there was no sign of him until later that afternoon when Faye went into her father's room to find the two of them playing chess. Alaric was scowling in a way that meant he was being beaten, which very rarely happened. "Don't say you've found your match at last?" Faye teased him as Jason moved in to checkmate.

"Certainly not, it was pure fluke," he declared loftily.

"Sure it is," Jason agreed. "And it was fluke that I won the last game, and the game before." He began to set up the board again, but Alaric stopped him.

"I feel much too tired for another game," he said, sounding suddenly faint. But since his eyes were twinkling nobody was alarmed. "I saved the local paper for you, darling," he said. "The theater has a visiting dance company that might interest you. It's called Dance Fiends."

"I don't think I've come across them before," she said, glancing at the advertisement. "It might be nice to have a night out."

"If you want to go I'll arrange seats," Jason said politely.

"Don't tell me you like the ballet?" Alaric twitted him.

"Yes. Ever since I had to keep a dancer under surveillance because of some very shady underworld dealings he was having on the side. I watched several of his performances, and I learned how very revealing of character movement can be. I've been fascinated by it ever since."

"As long as you don't confuse fantasy with reality," Faye said pointedly. "It's only a performance."

"Is it? I think people dance the way they are. It's as personal as handwriting," he said quietly.

Faye didn't reply to this. Jason was accusing her of trying to manipulate him, and it was a charge she couldn't totally deny.

Jason called the theater and discovered that there was a box free for that evening. Faye went to get ready, and descended an hour later in a cream silk dress cut on deceptively simple lines. He was waiting for her by the car.

When they were halfway to town he said abruptly, "I wish you'd forget the things I said to you this morning. They were completely out of line."

"Jason, I know how it must have seemed, but it wasn't like that. If you'd only let me explain—"

"But you don't owe me any explanations," he said quickly. "Your relationship with your fiancé is your own affair. I don't enter into it at all. Let's leave it like that, and try to have a good evening, shall we?"

"Of course," she said in a colorless voice.

When they parked the car he made a sign for her to stay where she was while he got out and looked up and down the street. When he was satisfied he opened her door and took her arm. His hand was warm against her bare skin and she braced herself against the pleasant shock.

He kept hold of her as they walked the few yards to the theater, and all the time she was aware of his body close to hers, of the movements of hard muscles beneath his clothes. The sensation of wanting him was so sharp that she had to take a deep breath. But the man who'd said the touch of her could make him shake seemed unaware of her now.

At the entrance to the theater Jason stopped abruptly and turned to look back the way they'd come, while his hand tightened on her arm. Faye followed his gaze but the busy street looked normal to her. "What is it?" she asked.

"The hairs on the back of my neck are standing up," he said. "When that happens it means someone's watching me. Maybe whoever's threatening you *does* know you're here, after all."

"I can't see anything strange," she said, cautiously. "It's a busy street. How can you tell?"

"Experience. Let's get inside."

It was still early so they went to the theater bar. Faye quickly diverted the conversation away from Jason's suspicions. She knew no one was watching them.

He was a punctilious host, consulting her wishes, ensuring that she wasn't sitting in a draft, but his barrier of perfect courtesy was impenetrable.

When they were in the box Faye looked around at the old-fashioned auditorium, filled with red plush and gilt. It was the first time she'd been in a theater since the accident that had ended her career, and the familiar sounds of an orchestra tuning up and the growing hum of an audience getting into its seats touched a responsive chord in her heart.

In spirit she was behind the curtain with the artists who were making frantic last-minute adjustments to their costumes, and touching their lucky mascots. A faint smile touched her lips as she recalled the tours she had made, the awkward stages and variable acoustics, the performances danced before a black curtain because the sets had gone to the wrong town. There were the good things, too, the camaraderie, the applause that had lifted her when she was tired, and the deep, private satisfaction, greater than any applause, of knowing that she'd given her best.

Tonight she wouldn't remember that *Carmen* had ended tragically. Instead she would think of Damien—no one had ever known his full name—the company's ferocious little choreographer, who'd created the work for her, and insisted on her dancing the lead despite the fury of the official leading lady. "No Faye, no *Carmen*," he'd said bluntly. And they'd gotten away with it.

Damien had looked past her pale English-rose beauty and discovered something deeply sensual in her nature that he'd exploited in his scorchingly erotic choreography. She'd played Carmen as a free spirit who'd taken men on her own terms, determined to bring Don José to her feet when he seemed indifferent, bored when he became possessive, defiant when he murdered her. And the audiences had loved her until...

As her smile faded she came out of her reverie and found Jason regarding her strangely. "Let's look at the program," she said hastily.

Three one-act works were scheduled for the evening. The first was a traditional nineteenth-century piece, but the second was *Mr. Punch*, a variation on Punch and Judy danced to an electronic score. "That makes me fear the worst," Jason observed grimly.

Faye nodded. "I know. 'Electronic score' is jargon for burps and belches. Let's just hope it's short."

As the lights went down a man came through the curtains and solemnly announced, "We regret that Mr. Quentin Davies, who was to have danced the role of the crocodile is indisposed. The crocodile will now be danced by Mr. Luther Welbeck."

"Luther!" Faye gave a quick, joyful exclamation. "Do you know him?"

"He was in the Kramer Ballet. I didn't know he'd left. But why didn't I see his name in the program?"

She scanned it again and finally located Luther's name buried in the corps de ballet. The sight saddened her. It was Luther who'd eased her way into the Kramer Ballet when she'd been a nervous sixteen-year-old. He'd been one of the company's stars, a character dancer of multifaceted brilliance, and to her eager young eyes he'd seemed on a level with the gods. Now he was an extra who understudied a crocodile.

Her sadness grew as she watched the ballet, which was hopelessly pretentious and devoid of inspiration. The crocodile was required to do little more than galumph around, totally wasting Luther's wit and gift for characterization. As the curtain fell she said, "I'd like to go backstage and say hello."

They made their way to the stage door and into a maze of corridors where dancers were milling around, still in costume. Faye saw Luther almost at once and waved to him. He waved back, his creased face split by a beaming grin, and in another moment they were clasped in each other's arms. "By jiminy, this is wonderful!" he yelped. "Faye! What are you doing here?"

"What are *you*? You were with Kramer when I last saw you."

"Ah, that's a long story. You look wonderful."

"Luther, this is Jason Royce, a friend of mine."

Luther was just below medium height and Jason had to look down at him. As he did so an old instinct, born in his early days on the force, started something tapping in his brain. Luther's eyes were full of laughter and he had a good deal of charm, rather as if a genial garden gnome had come to life. Plus he obviously adored Faye. Yet Jason had an uneasy feeling as if something had sideslipped. He shook Luther's hand, trying to sense him out through the physical contact, but he could detect nothing wrong. "Perhaps you could have a drink with us after the show?" he said pleasantly.

"Actually I usually leave now," Luther replied. "I wouldn't stay for the last piece if I were you. It's about two fellers rolling around the floor in string vests trying to discover the 'Meaning Of Life.'" Luther managed to suggest quotes and capitals by his manner, and Faye chuckled. He added with malicious relish, "One of them discovered a nail on the stage last night. It was the best entertainment anyone's had all week."

"You don't change," Faye said happily. "Let's go as soon as you're dressed."

Luther joined them half an hour later and they went into the theater bar. To Faye's relief her old friend saved her from embarrassment by being the first to refer to his new life. "So how the mighty have fallen, eh?" he intoned over a double whiskey.

"I remember you as the mightiest of the mighty," she said, squeezing his hand.

"Yeah, but *anno Domini* gets us all in the end, love. I'm past fifty, and not as spry as I was. But never mind that. Tell me about you. The last time I saw you it was in the hospital. S'trewth, but you looked a mess!"

"Why, what happened?" Jason asked.

"Don't you know? You mean Faye's never told you?"

"You tell me," Jason suggested, quietly refilling Luther's glass.

"I had an accident, that's all," Faye said. She was reluctant for Jason to hear about it, knowing that he saw her through a distorting mirror. With her career in ruins she'd become engaged to a rich man. It would look like the oldest story in the book.

"Tell me," Jason repeated to Luther. "How did this accident happen?"

"It weren't no accident," Luther said sourly. He assumed a satirical tone. "Mr. Roderick Manson, our dear and glorious leading man, was higher than a kite. He should have been given the push as soon as he started taking stuff, but not on your life. Cyril, the company director, was potty about him, and he wasn't going to banish the love of his life, was he?

"So, one night Faye's performing *Carmen*, with 'darling Roddy,' who's somewhere in the stratosphere. He hoists her over his head and pitches her straight down into the orchestra pit. Screams and hysteria, Roddy weeping all over Cyril's shoulder, Cyril promising him it'll be all right, and Faye wakes up in the hospital with a month's pay and a note saying, 'Ta very much, but don't come back.' It was a ruddy scandal. And you should have seen the way she looked, white as a sheet and her head wrapped in bandages."

"Those flowers you sent did a lot for me," Faye put in before Jason could say anything.

"Yeah, well, you were always my favorite girlfriend." Luther patted her hand. "I'd have liked to come and see you again but the company moved on. You know how it was. Anyway, enough of that. What's been happening to you since? Are you dancing yet?"

"No, I—I haven't done any dancing since then."

"But you still practice?"

"I try."

"What are you doing in this neck of the woods?"

"I'm staying nearby, in a house owned by my fiancé."

"You got engaged? That's terrific. Anyone I know?"

"His name's Conroy Niall."

Luther chuckled. "Same name as that millionaire bloke. You know the one I mean, rat-faced little git who buys newspapers faster than I buy socks and turns them all into girlie mags."

"Since when have you minded that?" Faye teased him. "I couldn't look into your dressing room without getting an eyeful."

"I didn't say I had anything against it," Luther explained patiently, "but what I say is we need *some* quality press—otherwise how would we get the sports reports?"

"You're incorrigible," Faye laughed. It gave her a feeling of pleasure to know that her old friend's sharp tongue hadn't deserted him, as though in a shifting world she'd found the one thing that would never change. "Actually," she went on carefully, "my fiancé owns a few newspapers."

Luther's face was a study. "You don't mean—? It's not—? Ah, c'mon, Faye, you can't do this to me. It's not the same bloke, is it?"

"I'm afraid it is," she said, enjoying his look of comic horror.

"You mean you're going to get hitched to that handsome, distinguished-looking feller who's done so much to bring standards and good taste back to the communications industry?" Luther asked, recovering himself admirably.

Faye laughed. "That's the one."

"Well I'll be—" He regarded her with admiration. "You got yourself a millionaire? Good for you, luv. There aren't that many around. Grab one when he passes, 'cos he won't pass again." Seeing Faye wince he backtracked hastily, "Don't take any notice of me. I'm just pig vulgar. I know you're not like that. It's just that if true love is going to strike, it's nice if it can strike in the right place, if you see what I mean."

"Of course," she said hastily.

"So how's your dad? I remember his coming to re-hearsals."

"Dad's not too well. He had a heart attack recently. That's why we've come out here, so that he can recover quietly. Luther, why don't you come and have lunch with us? I'm sure he'd love to see you again."

"Fine. Just tell me when."

"How about tomorrow?"

"You're on."

They said their goodbyes. Jason, who'd sat quietly watching them for the past few minutes, told Luther he'd be waiting for him at the main gate of Haverill Manor, and then drew Faye away. He studied the street carefully before letting her come out, but whoever he thought he'd seen earlier was gone now. Faye wondered if he would ask her about what he'd heard that night but he drove home in thoughtful silence, and bid her a brief good-night.

Before he went to bed, Jason called up Jerry Atkins, an old friend from the police force. When the greetings were out of the way he said, "I'd be grateful if you'd run something through the computer for me. The name is Luther Welbeck. He's a dancer, used to be with the Kramer Ballet. He left recently."

"It doesn't ring any bells."

"I doubt he's a real crook, but he might be doing small stuff. Or I might be wrong. It's just a feeling I have."

"Okay. Will do. Call me tomorrow."

Chapter Nine

Alaric was delighted at the thought of a guest for lunch. Faye had to insist on his taking a rest in the morning, something he resisted as determinedly as a recalcitrant child. Jason left them arguing and went to use the phone in the breakfast room.

"I've run Welbeck through the computer and he's pretty clean," Jerry told him. "He's kept some dubious company now and then, largely because he's a bit too fond of blowing his pay at racetracks, but he's never been caught at anything criminal. It's odd you should mention the Kramer Ballet, though, because we've had our eye on them recently. Roddy Manson's had an expensive habit for some time."

"So why didn't you pull him in months ago?" Jason demanded angrily.

"Because we suspect he's financing it by pushing and we're hoping he'll lead us to bigger fish."

"In the meantime he's free to cause a hell of a lot of damage to the other dancers," Jason observed grimly. "Their safety doesn't matter, I suppose?"

"Can't be helped. Sometimes these things are necessary, you know that. It's a matter of long-term strategy."

"To hell with long-term strategy," Jason snapped, and slammed down the phone.

A movement behind him made him turn. He found Faye staring at him with a puzzled frown. "I heard what you said," she told him. "You were talking to your police friends, weren't you—about Roddy?"

"Yes. But why does that bother you? Won't it please you to know that he's going to be put away where he deserves?"

"To be frank, yes. But that's not the point. When Luther told you about him he didn't know you were an ex-policeman."

"What difference does that make? Anyway, I didn't betray Luther's confidence, if that's what you think. The police already have Roddy Manson on file. I called them to run a check on Luther."

She stared. "Why?"

"Because something about him worries me— something I just don't trust."

"That's outrageous," she flared. "Luther is the kindest man in the world. He made the company give me a start, and he taught me how to survive. I was fresh out of dancing school and all I knew was how to put one foot in front of the other. He taught me how to *act*, and it made all the difference. I owe him so much and when I think I introduced him to you, and you went checking up on him behind his back..."

"Have you finished?" he demanded coldly. He had a strange sense of hurt. He'd been indignant and protective on her behalf and this was all the thanks he got.

"I suppose so. I hope I've made my feelings plain."

"Very. And let me say that knowing you learned your considerable acting skills from Luther Welbeck doesn't make me think any better of him."

"You know nothing about my acting skills."

"I thought I'd had an excellent demonstration of them."

"Don't try to change the subject. Just tell me—what dreadful deeds have you pinned on him? Has he been running a white-slave racket in the intervals of being a dancer?"

"He hasn't got a criminal record—"

"Of course he hasn't. The very idea is nonsense."

"If you say so, I must have been wrong."

Something in his tone made her look at him shrewdly and say, "You're just saying that. You don't really think you were wrong."

"All right, no I don't. My instincts are telling me bad things about him."

"That's not your instincts. It's your determination to think the worst at all times. But not everyone in this world is on the take, Jason, whatever you think. Luther is a kind, good man, and he's my friend. I'm asking you to be polite to him today."

"You're very fierce in his defense," he said coldly. "You don't give me any credit for knowing what I'm talking about or wanting to protect you."

"Protect me? But that's silly—" she broke off and amended quickly "—it's silly to think I could need protecting from Luther."

"Then there's no more to be said." Jason walked off, leaving her staring after him and wondering about an air of suppressed pain in his manner.

At one o'clock she saw Jason heading for the car and ran to join him. He drove to the main gate and they sat waiting for Luther to appear. When he did he was on foot. "You haven't walked all the way?" Faye demanded, scandalized.

"No, I took the bus. It's not a long walk from the stop and it did me good," he said cheerily.

"But what happened to your car?"

"I had a bit of an accident with it. And I'd delayed getting the new insurance, so that was that."

And perhaps even a taxi might strain his budget now, Faye thought sadly, remembering the vintage Rolls-Royce that had been Luther's pride and joy. It had been the only material possession he'd cared for. Apart from his car he'd declared that dancing and the company of his friends were all he needed, and his life proclaimed it to be true. She squeezed his hand and felt him squeeze back.

He stared out the windows on the short drive to the house and uttered a soft "Blimey!" as the extent of the grounds became plain to him. "Is that the house?" he asked suddenly, pointing to a building almost hidden by trees that lay along their way.

"No, that's the pavilion," Jason informed him. "I believe the last owner renovated it but never used it."

"Do you mean the Arab sheikh?" Faye asked.

"That's the one."

"What's it like inside?" Luther asked. "Full of silk curtains and eastern latticework?"

"I don't know," Faye replied. "I've never seen it. It looks interesting."

"We can look if you like," Jason said and turned the car.

The pavilion was the size of a small house and the inside made them stare. It was luxuriously furnished with a huge bed covered in a thick fur rug and a bathroom with gold-plated taps. To Luther's fiendish delight the walls were decorated with hangings of exotic design. He grinned. "Fancy having a garden shed like this!"

"It's a bit—ostentatious," Faye said hesitantly.

"More than a bit, love. It's like a stage set. And he never used it?"

"I believe he only spent two months at Haverill Manor in the entire five years he owned it," Jason explained.

They looked around for a little longer before returning to the car. After a few minutes Jason deposited them at the front door. Alaric came out and greeted Luther robustly.

As the weather was hot Martha had laid a table outside on the terrace where there was the best view of the grounds. To Faye's relief there were five places. She was afraid Jason might have made some excuse.

But when they all sat down to lunch and Jason assiduously engaged Luther in conversation it dawned on Faye that she'd underrated him. Jason seemed deeply absorbed in the details of Luther's life, barely uttering a word except to make encouraging noises. Actually, as Faye quickly realized, he was simply giving Luther a long rope and hoping he would hang himself.

"You know quite a bit about ballet, don't you?" Luther said at last. "Funny, I wouldn't have had you down as a bloke who'd care for it."

"He doesn't, really," Faye put in before Jason could answer. "It's a standard police technique, keeping quiet and letting other people talk, isn't it, Jason?"

"You a copper then?" Luther queried, looking mildly interested.

"I was once," Jason said briefly. "Not now."

"Don't be so modest, Jason," Faye said, looking at him with an angry smile. "Once a copper, always a copper. It's an attitude of mind, isn't it?"

"If you mean by that that an ex-policeman doesn't stop being interested in people, I suppose you're right," Jason said quietly.

"No, that's not what I meant." Faye was tempted to tell Luther that she'd caught Jason checking up on him that morning. But then she caught Jason's eye and something in his expression told her that he'd read her intention and was forbidding her to do it. For a moment they fought a silent battle. Then her eyes fell. It annoyed her to realize that he'd won, he'd imposed his will on her by sheer force of personality. She became aware that Luther was saying something.

"When I was a kid I wanted to be a copper," he was recalling. "But I wasn't big enough. So it had to be dancing." They all laughed and Luther turned to Alaric. "I remember you had some ambitions in that direction, Mr. Stafford."

"Dad? A dancer?" Faye queried, puzzled.

"No, he had an idea for a ballet," Luther explained. "He told me about it once when he was visiting you at rehearsal. It was a good notion, too. Damien thought it had great possibilities."

Faye turned to Alaric. "You never told me this," she reproached him.

"I wanted to work out something definite, darling. I thought I might surprise you. But somehow it never happened."

"What would it have been about?"

"Variations on the theme of medieval chivalry, set to the music of some old troubadour songs. It would have been a celebration of the days when a knight would become a lady's champion, willing to do anything she asked in return for a word and a smile." Alaric spoke with relish, inwardly enjoying the triumph he might have had. "That was a glorious time and we ought to remind ourselves of it sometimes."

"It sounds lovely," Faye said enthusiastically.

Luther's voice crackled with laughter and he pointed at Jason. "There's one bloke who doesn't think so," he chortled.

"I'm sorry," Jason said hastily, conscious that his face had betrayed him. "I didn't mean to be rude, but to me it sounds like fantasy. People like to sentimentalize about the golden days of chivalry but they never existed. The heroic knights were thugs on the make, and none of them ever did anything for so little as a word and a smile."

"Nonsense. You're forgetting that people had only just discovered the power of romantic love," Alaric said, plunging into the argument with relish. "That's something you should never underestimate. But I suppose since you're the product of a cynical age you don't believe in it. More fool you!"

Jason grinned. "I certainly don't believe in any power strong enough to make me fight a dragon merely to please 'my lady.' I like to choose my own dragons and fight them for my own reasons."

Alaric groaned theatrically. "I don't know what young men are coming to. Wouldn't your pains be rewarded by the touch of her lily-white hand?"

"Not unless it contained a large check," Jason said, and they all laughed. But Faye's laughter died quickly. By a strange irony Alaric had summed up exactly what she'd been planning to do—ask Jason to be her champion. And now she knew what kind of answer she could expect if she were foolish enough to try.

"It's a lovely idea," she told Alaric wistfully.

He sighed. "It was just a whim. But I used to enjoy thinking about seeing you dance the lead, darling."

Luther nodded. "Faye was headed right for the top. Still—" he looked around, taking in the luxurious mansion and the beautiful grounds "—as one door closes another one opens, eh? This is nothing to sniff at."

"It's all happened for the best," Alaric said quickly. "Things usually do happen for the best in the long run."

Faye said nothing and seemed to be absorbed in her food. But Jason was watching her face, and he was startled. In the last split second before she blanked out all expression he saw a look of utter misery. It was gone in a flash but he was sure of what he'd seen, and what it meant. Whatever the others might say, Faye didn't think it was for the best. He wondered if he would ever understand her.

When the meal was over Faye touched Luther's arm and said quietly, "There's something I want you to see."

She took him to the top of the house and showed him the gymnasium. "This is where I practice," she said. "I haven't given in, even now."

"Good for you," he said at once. He saw her anxious face and read her thoughts accurately. "Don't take any notice of the things I say, love. I told you I was vulgar. At my age security looks good. But it's different when you're young. Are you going to go on dancing when you're married?"

"Conroy and I haven't discussed it," she said carefully.

"But you still want to follow that star, don't you?" He hugged her. "You go for it, then."

She smiled in relief. For a moment Luther hadn't seemed to understand, but he'd recovered and shown that he was still her dear friend.

Jason was waiting for them by the car. "I'll take you all the way back," he said courteously to Luther. "Faye, will you come?"

"No, I'll stay here," she said. She kissed Luther goodbye, promised to see him again and stood watching as the car vanished down the driveway. As soon as it was out of sight she raced back up to her room and hastily changed into her practice gear of black tights and pink shirt. Then she returned to the gymnasium. Luther's words, "You still want to follow that star, don't you?" had fired her. Now was the time to confront her demons and defeat them.

One of the walls of the gymnasium was lined with climbing bars, arranged in sections that could be swung free at one end. She pulled out the end of one section and secured it to the floor. Then she confronted it, her heart hammering. After a few deep breaths she began to climb.

As she went higher the old terrors began again but she forced herself on. When she was ten feet high she glanced down but all she could see was the orchestra pit rushing up to meet her and she quickly looked away again. Slowly she descended. She wasn't beaten yet. There was still something she could do.

Some thick landing mats were rolled up in a corner. She hauled one out and laid it at the foot of the bars, then fetched another and laid it on top. Now if she fell she would have a soft landing, and this knowledge would give her confidence. She began to climb again.

But this time it was worse. Having already failed once made it harder. Her legs seemed weighed down by lead. She hauled herself up to fifteen feet, then another step, and another, telling herself not to look down. She stopped with her arms hooked over a bar. Her heart thundered against her ribs. She tried to reason with herself. She was being ridiculous. She wasn't very high and there was a mat to fall on. But the little voice of common sense was drowned out by the repetition of the nightmare. Once she'd been utterly fearless. Now terror held her trapped without even the strength to move.

When she finally made the attempt she found herself instinctively looking down and had to close her eyes. Keeping them closed she tried again, found a lower rung by touch, tested it, put her weight on it. Then the other foot, and so on, carefully, until she reached the ground. She was in despair. Her last hope had gone and the whole lonely battle suddenly seemed futile. She rested her head against the upright, too drained to do anything but stay there, and felt her courage fail her. Tears slipped from beneath her eyelids and she no longer had the will to fight them.

She felt a soft touch on her hair and looked up to find Jason beside her. "I didn't know you were back," she said hastily, brushing her hand across her face.

"I came in a few minutes ago. I've been watching you. You were trying to overcome your fear, weren't you?"

"Yes."

"And when you couldn't, you . . ." He touched her wet face. "Does it matter so much?" he asked gently.

"Yes, it matters," she said. "I've lost my nerve. I don't know how to get it back, but I *must*."

"Your career means that much to you?" he asked curiously.

"Dancing was more than a career to me. It isn't just what I do, it's what I *am*. Now I'm stranded in a dreadful limbo. I couldn't even fight to make the company take me back because while I'm like this I've got nothing to offer. I'm useless."

"That's nonsense," he said, giving her a curious look.

"Don't talk about it. You can't know," she told him passionately. "When Roddy lifted me he was standing near the edge of the stage. He held me up high, with my head hanging down, looking straight into the orchestra pit and when I fell—it was such a long way down—I keep seeing it."

"So you come here to fight it. But it can't work, Faye. You're going about it the wrong way."

"Then what's the right way?" she demanded.

"This," he said simply, and moved so fast that she never saw it. The next moment she was thrown up into the air. Jason's arms were at full stretch over his head and his large hands were grasping her firmly by the hips, suspending her in space.

"Put me down," she gasped.

He didn't move. His arms were like steel bars, holding her without tremor. His head was thrown back so that he could meet her eyes, and his own eyes were brilliant. "If I put you down, you're finished. You know that, don't you?" he challenged. "You were dropped by a man and you need to be held up safely by a man. That's the only thing that'll give you back your confidence."

Faye reached out for the bars but Jason immediately turned away from them, moving easily while he held her one-hundred-and-two-pound body above his head. The air seemed to whirl around her. "Put me down," she managed to say again.

"What's the matter?" he jeered. "Scared?"

"You know I am," she cried.

"No, I don't mean that. I mean scared that someone's going to call your bluff."

"What bluff?"

"The pretense that you want to work at regaining your old talent—your old self. She was a brilliant self, that other woman. She could scorch across a stage and bring the audience's dreams to life. She was someone worth being. And she worked her head off in a way that Conroy Niall's woman will never have to. So you lost your nerve. What a lovely excuse! How convenient!"

"It's true," she screamed.

"But it doesn't have to go on being true. I'm offering you the best chance you'll ever have and you don't want to take it, do you?"

His eyes held hers hypnotically. The world seemed to steady around her. But she knew if she shifted her gaze to the ground everything would start spinning again. "Yes," she said at last. "I want to take it."

"Then it has to be this way. I can hold you up as long as I have to—and I won't let you fall. You know that, don't you?"

"I don't . . . know . . . anything."

"Then think. Concentrate your thoughts to where I'm holding you. Feel my hands. Don't they feel strong, Faye?"

"Yes," she breathed.

"I'll never fail you. Keep reminding yourself of that. I'm going to bring you down for a brief rest. Then we'll start again."

He bent his arms and Faye felt herself descending slowly. He lowered her inch by inch so that she touched the ground gently. Every limb was weak and she clung to him. Jason tightened his arm around her waist and held her against him. "Steady now," he said.

Faye became aware that his shirt was open and his chest was rising and falling. But an answering instinct inside told her that it wasn't the strain of lifting her that made him breathe like that. Looking up, she saw the naked need in his eyes, but in the same instant his face became taut as though he'd imposed control on himself by force. "Tell me what you want, Faye," he said in a harsh voice.

"I want—to be myself again," she said.

"And you want that far more than you want any man, don't you?" he demanded in a tone that might have been self-mockery.

"Right this minute, yes."

"Lie down." He drew her down onto the mat, turned her over and began to rub her spine. "You're full of tension. We've got to get rid of that. Relax."

He pulled on her shirt until the ends came apart and he could slide his hands beneath. But his touch on her bare skin was impersonal as he massaged her skillfully. "Where did you learn to do that?" she murmured.

"From the police physiotherapist. I've had a few injuries in my time. I found it's always the same muscles that go first."

"Yes," she said, feeling instantly at home with his understanding. "With me it's the small of my back that aches before anything else."

He knelt astride her legs and began to work on the small of her back, kneading it with his thumbs so that it warmed and eased. She might have imagined the blazing desire she'd seen in his eyes only a moment ago. He was devoting himself to her service, infusing her aching muscles with a heat that was merely comfortable. "All right," he said after a while. "Now we'll try again."

He swung her up before she could protest, and this time it was easier. She forced herself to look down at the floor and discovered, with dawning excitement, that it stayed in its proper place. It wasn't an orchestra pit full of sharp objects, it was just a floor. "Don't stretch your arms out in that defensive way," Jason ordered her. "It looks as if you're expecting to fall."

She drew her arms back and held them at her sides. If she fell now there was nothing between her head and the floor. But with sudden thrilling certainty she knew she wasn't going to fall. The arms that supported her could always hold her safe.

Gradually Jason returned her to the ground. The sight of her face startled him. It was flushed and her eyes had a new glitter. "Are you all right?" he asked.

"I'm going to be," she said in an intense tone he'd never heard her use before. "But there's one more thing. In the dance I took a flying leap toward Roddy—"

"—and he caught you while you were soaring over his head," Jason finished. "I remember that moment. It was spectacular. When we've worked some more we'll try it."

"I want to try it now," she said.

"No, Faye, it's a tricky move."

"That's what it's all about. This is my chance, Jason. I have to do it *now*—or it'll be too late."

"Suppose I miss you?"

"You won't." When he still frowned she reminded him, "You told me to trust you."

He began to understand the glitter in her eyes. He'd challenged her and she'd accepted the challenge. Now she was turning it around on him, and it scared him. "You'd really place that kind of faith in me?" he asked quietly.

"I know I can."

"Only if we practice slowly first."

"We will," Faye assured him, and he realized that she'd taken charge.

She walked away to take up position, and while he waited his own words over lunch came back to him like a mocking echo. He'd repudiated the idea of chivalry, but now he was as ready to obey her commands as any lovesick knight trying to earn his lady's favor. There was no "large check" in this for him, only the need to see the trouble vanish from Faye's face. But that need had submerged all others. Even the craving to make love to her, which tormented him constantly, was in abeyance before the conviction that only her happiness mattered.

She came leaping toward him, and he caught her at head height. They did it a couple of times before she said, in a voice of authority, "Now I'm going to come at you fast. Let me go high before you catch me."

She went to the far side of the gymnasium, stood to take a deep breath, and began to run toward him, gathering speed for the final leap that took her high into the air. There was a split second of fear as she launched herself into space, then the feel of his hands on her hips, holding her steady. She raised one leg, tilting the balance of her body so that her head hung down. She stayed there for a long moment while the arms supporting her never moved. And the nightmare was over.

"Faye..." Jason said anxiously.

"I'm all right," she said in a strange, quiet voice. "Let me down now."

He began to lower her. When she could grip his shoulders he let her slide slowly through his hands until he was holding her waist. Looking up at her he said, "*Tell* me! Did we do it?"

Faye cupped his face between her hands. "Yes," she said. "Oh, Jason, we did it."

He lowered her further, bringing their faces closer together and she clasped him tightly, fastening her mouth on his in joy and triumph. She kissed him wildly, trying to show him, not just her dawning love, but the liberation of spirit he'd helped her rediscover. She'd been earthbound but now she could soar again. It was Jason who had brought this about and in return he could have everything she was. This was what her lips were silently telling him.

He continued to hold her up so that her mouth was above his. He was enjoying the sensation of being thoroughly and dramatically kissed. She was almost ruthless in her determination to impose her caresses on him and he stood there in a spin of delight for what felt like a long time. "We did it," she was murmuring. "We did it . . . do you hear . . . ? we did it . . ."

"I hear—" he gasped, but fell silent as her tongue took possession of his mouth, seeking out the dark warmth within and sending such violent tremors through him that he was afraid of dropping her. Without taking his mouth from hers he scooped her up into his arms, then knelt down and gently lowered her to the mat. He lay with her beneath him while her lips still worked their enchantment.

They'd reached this point before, but this time they both knew there was no turning back. The force that held them in its thrall was the force of life itself, and they'd denied it too long. Now it burst forth irresistibly, making their bodies strain with the desire to be one.

Faye was exploring the promise of his mouth, provoking it with her own. He answered her with enthusiasm, plunging deep into her with his tongue, hinting at future delight. Each flickering probe sent ripples of pleasure through her, trailing off only to start again at the center and expand into infinity. The sensual shape of his lips had told a true story; he knew how to use them to please and tease a woman.

Jason tugged at the ends of her shirt until it opened and her breasts were bared, the nipples already taut with desire. He tore open his own shirt and leaned down to rain kisses over her face. The feel of his bare chest against her skin was electrifying, and she moaned, clasping her hands in his hair with abandon.

He dropped his lips to her neck, trailing down its length and flicking his tongue over her skin in a way that made little noises of pleasure emerge from deep within her. "I've wanted to kiss you here," he murmured hoarsely. His mouth touched the hollow of her throat, "Just here..."

She gasped and shuddered from the sensations that rioted through her. But immediately they were superseded by other sensations as he touched her breasts. His caress was feather light, tantalizing, and everything in her yearned to surrender to the promise implicit in his touch. But first they both needed patience to discover each other slowly. Only then would they be ready to sound the depths of the feeling that drew them so irresistibly together.

Faye knew that this would be different from what any other man could give her. Until now dancing had been the first love of her life, and men had always come second. Her few romances had foundered on the rock of the man's jealousy of her dedication to her work. But Jason, instead of being jealous, had returned her first love to her with generous hands. Now he would always be a part of it, and it of him, and loving one meant loving the other.

He dropped his head and began to caress one soft, full breast with his lips and tongue, leaving trails of fire behind each flickering touch. "Yes..." Faye murmured, "oh, yes..."

He'd reached the peaked nipple, and suddenly he darted his tongue across it in a rasping movement that seared through her and made her moan with poignant pleasure. He did it again, and then again, while Faye arched beneath him, wondering if she would go out of her mind with ecstasy.

"I wanted to be sure you really wanted me," he whispered in her ear.

"And what have you decided?" she managed to ask.

"I think you do."

"I think I'll die if you don't make love to me."

He answered by dropping a hand to her waist and sliding a couple of fingers beneath the waistband of her tights. Still moving tentatively he eased his hand downward. Faye sighed at how good his touch felt against her bare skin. She wanted to remove all barriers between them as quickly as possible and be naked against him, but she controlled her impatience and let him take control. Jason was touching her with a loving reverence that told her he wanted to make it perfect.

He curled the fingers of his other hand over the top of her tights and began to ease them gently down over her hips, then down her long slender legs. As her pale skin came into view, inch by inch, she felt first the shock of the cool air, then a burning sensitivity when she saw the craving in his eyes as they lingered on her.

Unable to remain still, Faye reached for his belt buckle. While she worked on it he unfastened the buttons of his shirt and yanked it off. His jeans came off next and he lay down beside her, taking her into his arms and covering her face and neck with hot, urgent kisses. Faye rejoiced from the feel of them but she wanted more. She'd seen the hard power of his arousal and a throbbing deep within told her that she'd waited too long for what this man could give. She pressed against him and felt the sudden weight as he moved over her, parting her legs gladly, eager to know the fulfillment of his passion.

He possessed her, and she was overwhelmed with a glorious sense of completeness. The fear and tension that had tormented her seemed to fall away. Now there was only a wonderful knowledge that everything was right, that she was doing something that had been written in her stars. She belonged here, in this man's arms, looking up into his face and seeing there the mirror of her thoughts.

Jason began moving slowly but when he saw the radiant happiness on her face he thrust harder, entering her deeply. The feeling of being encompassed by her was more wonderful than anything he had ever known, and somehow sensation became fused with emotion, so that loving her and making love to her became the same. Feverishly he wondered if it was the same with her, or if the blissful expression on her face was only the reflection of what had happened earlier. Even now, when he felt so close to her, he didn't really know her. "Faye..." he groaned.

"Yes...my dearest...again, again...." Her words ended in a luxurious sigh and she arched against him, telling him wordlessly what she wanted. He'd lit a fire inside her and now it was raging, melting her, merging her with him. Gradually, inexorably, the time was coming when the miracle that possessed her would explode into nothingness. She tried to defer the moment, but it was impossible. Pleasure mounted within her, carrying her on a giddy spiral of desire. She cried out and her voice mingled with Jason's as her ecstasy peaked, sending shudders of brilliant sensation through her body. They clung to each other as the intensity faded, and Faye was left drained of everything except a deep sense of fulfillment.

She lay with Jason in her arms while her heartbeat slowed and she was held silent by a sense of wonder. In the last split second she'd had a revelation like a flash of lightning. Jason was the man for her. Everything was so clear now that she could only wonder why she had never seen it before. Her heart had known it soon enough, but she'd been afraid to face it. For all her plans and schemes, the truth was that she'd been seeking love from the only man whose love she could ever want.

Chapter Ten

Faye, I'm going to ask you something, and I want you to tell me honestly. It's important.''

She kissed him. "What is it, darling?"

He didn't reply immediately. Instead he got up from the bed and went to the window. A half full wine bottle and two glasses stood on the sill. They were in the pavilion they'd explored on the day of Luther's visit, the day they'd finally found each other. It felt like a lifetime ago, but in fact it was only two days. In that short time they'd revelled in the joy of their love, escaping to the pavilion where they could know peace and privacy, and discovering the world in each other's hearts and bodies.

Now, suffused in the languorous content that always followed Jason's loving, Faye lay back and watched his movements. He was magnificently naked, his long limbs and hard, lean body bathed in the mellow light that filtered through the blinds. The sight of his taut, muscular thighs reminded her of the steely power that lay there, power that enabled him to thrust deeply into her again and again, bury himself completely inside her. The world seemed far away at this moment.

He brought the glasses back to the bed and handed one to her. "What do you want to know?" she asked again, for he seemed to have trouble finding a place to start.

"When we first met—" Jason played with her fingers, seeming to find that easier than looking at her "—did you know I was the man who could help you?" he asked at last. "Was that all you wanted?"

Faye was glad he wasn't looking at her face. The shock that must be revealed on it would tell him too much. She felt a pit opening at her feet. "What . . . exactly do you mean by that?" she asked cautiously.

"I mean, did you know I could help you get your nerve back? Did you look at me and say, 'He's got strong arms. He can help me become a dancer again.' Was that all it was? Because I couldn't bear to think that I was just a means to an end."

For a moment relief held her frozen. Then, picking her words carefully, she said, "I swear to you that it never crossed my mind that you could help overcome my fear of heights."

"Of course it didn't," he said quickly, in a voice of self-disgust. "Forgive me, my darling. I don't know what came over me to ask you such a question. But I'm a devil these days. I suspect everyone. Try not to think too badly of me."

Faye looked at him in dismay, sickened by her own words. She'd told him the literal truth, yet it was a dishonest kind of truth. For she'd sought him out with an ulterior motive in one way, if not in another, and now she knew how he would regard the deception that had seemed so innocent in the beginning. His eyes shone with love and trust, and suddenly she couldn't look at him anymore.

"Don't turn away," he begged. "Have I really offended you? I know it's a lot to ask you to understand what makes me like this, but—"

"I do understand," she said quickly, unable to bear his apologies, which made her feel guiltier with every second. "And even if I didn't, I'd still love you, Jason. Whatever you did, it would make no difference. If you love someone enough, nothing else matters. You can overlook anything even if—even if you think it's terribly wrong." She took his face between her hands and spoke in a voice that trembled with earnestness as she tried to convey a message that perhaps he'd remember when the time came. "Perhaps that's what love is—understanding when you don't really understand at all."

"That's too deep for me," he said. "If you forgive me that's all I need."

"But I don't forgive you," she said passionately. "You don't need forgiveness for what you can't help."

"God bless you," he said with a new intensity in his voice. He buried his face between her breasts and lay there, resting against her, as though he'd suddenly found peace. After a while he murmured, "Do you realize what you said?"

"What did I say?"

"You said you loved me."

"Haven't I said it before?"

"No, I've been listening for it."

"Perhaps if you'd said it first . . ." she mentioned.

He lifted his head. "Do you need me to say I love you, Faye?"

It was there shining in his eyes and Faye drew in her breath, overwhelmed by the sight of his adoration. When he dropped his head against her soft warmth she instinctively enclosed him in her arms.

Jason, who'd known little tenderness in his life, felt the protectiveness in the gesture, and a kind of incredulous wonder ran through him. He'd never sought protection from anyone nor felt the need of it. But he wanted this woman's protection, and he sensed in her a profundity of secrets that he needed to unravel. There were things she could teach him that it had become very important to learn. He smiled suddenly.

"What is it?" Faye asked, feeling the smile against her breasts.

"Oddly enough I was thinking about your friend Luther, what he said about rolling around in string vests looking for the meaning of life." He looked up at her, smiling in a way that was almost impish. "I could tell you the meaning of life without having to wear a string vest."

She laughed, delighted with the nearest thing to a joke she'd ever heard from him. "There's no need," she replied. "I know the meaning of life. It's this."

"Yes," he said with a sigh of contentment. "It's this. It isn't even passion, although that comes into it."

"It certainly does," she murmured satirically, with a vibrant memory of the last couple of hours.

He shook with laughter, but almost immediately became serious again. "But it's more than that. If we couldn't make love—if you were ill, say—I could live without that as long as I could still lie here as we are now, listening to your heartbeat."

His words moved her profoundly. This big man, to whom the physical life was so vital, had offered her a side of himself that she guessed no one else knew about. And he'd hit on a truth she'd been trying to put into words. It wasn't merely passion that united them. The phrase "falling in love" didn't begin to describe it. They'd caught each other by the heart, and for good or ill they were interwoven with each other. She was about to tell him this when a slight sound made her look down. She found him asleep in her arms, and this, perhaps more than anything else, seemed to her to sum up the reality at the heart of their love.

Perhaps, after all, her fears were groundless. The man who loved her this much would understand and forgive when she told him everything. She would tell him—soon. All she asked was to spend a little longer with him in this cocooned heaven.

She dozed off, too, and they awoke together an hour later, smiling at each other. "Shall I tell you something?" she asked.

A glint of mischief deep in her eyes warned him to ask cautiously, "What?"

"I could eat a horse."

"And they say women are the romantic sex," he grumbled, rolling off the bed.

"I haven't had anything to eat since last night," she complained. She got up and put her jeans and shirt on. "I couldn't swallow any breakfast because I was thinking about spending today here with you."

"Same here."

"Well, I wouldn't know since you're still keeping your distance in the kitchen."

"Darling, if we eat together I'll never take my eyes off you. Until we're ready to tell the world about us it's best to play it safe. Personally I'd like to tell everyone now..." He left the sentence hanging in the air, but Faye shook her head.

"We can't. Not yet. For one thing we should wait until we're away from here."

"You're right. And there's your father to think of. He's set on your marrying money, isn't he? I've been able to deduce that much. I suppose when a man has come close to death he worries more about his daughter's security. But sooner or later he's got to understand that—no, I made a resolution not to badger you about this." He kissed her. "Let's not spoil our perfect day. I'll go see about coffee."

"Mmm, lovely."

He opened the bedroom door and nearly fell over Buck, who was stretched out on the other side. The dog looked up at him reproachfully, then turned his gaze on Faye.

"Poor old boy," she chuckled. "He's feeling neglected. Come here." She patted the bed and he leaped up beside her, flopping down with an immense sigh and rolling over to have his tummy rubbed. Faye obliged and Buck closed his eyes blissfully.

"He likes that," Jason observed, returning from the kitchen after he'd put the coffee on.

"Of course he does," Faye crooned. "He enjoys having a fuss made of him, don't you, old fellow?" She hugged him, growling deep in her throat. Buck growled back happily and they played together, arms and paws flailing in a canine version of pat-a-cake.

"He's like a little kid with you," Jason said, grinning. "I've always regarded him as a rather serious-minded dog."

"Perhaps he's had to be too serious-minded. Fun is good for him," Faye asserted.

It occurred to Jason that the same might be said about himself. He couldn't remember when he'd last felt so lighthearted, so cut off from the world's cares. He knew that soon the day of decisions would come, when problems must be faced, but he felt confident enough to cope with them. Nothing could go wrong while he had Faye's love. He stood there, watching her tenderly as she romped with the animal who could have snapped her like a twig, yet who was as gentle as a baby because he loved her.

When Faye was seated at the kitchen table with Buck's nose on her knee Jason protested, "He's not allowed to beg."

"I guess that's another of the things he's forgotten," Faye said serenely, offering Buck a piece of sausage, which vanished in one gulp.

"All this soft living is bad for him. He ought to be getting some proper exercise."

"Whose fault is it that he isn't?" Faye demanded. "How can he get a good run when his master spends all his time in dalliance?"

"That's true. We ought to take him out."

"As soon as we've finished eating," Faye declared.

Buck promptly thumped the ground with his tail and Faye obliged with another piece of sausage. Jason held out the plate with the remaining sausage and she ate it, smiling her thanks.

"I always thought dancers ate like birds," he observed, watching her with amusement.

"Actually most of them eat like horses. I certainly do when I'm practicing. It's a big drain on your energy."

"Shall I cook you another egg?"

"Yes, please," she said so quickly that he laughed.

When they were ready to go out Jason put on a light jacket with a deep pocket into which he could fit his cellular telephone. It was this phone that enabled Faye to slip away with a clear conscience. Although no one knew where they were, Don could call them if Alaric became ill. They were only a few minutes from the house, but the wood that surrounded the pavilion gave them complete privacy, and for all anyone knew they might have vanished from the face of the earth.

As soon as they were outside Buck dashed around joyfully, seeming not to know which way to run first. They laughed at his excitement and tried throwing the ball for him, but it kept getting lost in the undergrowth, so at last Faye put it in her pocket and Buck concentrated on exploring the thousand wonderful smells that surrounded him. "He had the best nose on the force," Jason said proudly as they walked with their arms entwined. "He could root out anything—drugs, explosives, nothing got past him."

"How's his retraining going?"

"Mostly we're managing all right."

The uneasy note in his voice made her glance up at him. "What about the gun?"

"He's as scared of guns as ever. He's always been so brave that I thought he'd be getting over it by now."

"I don't think it's a question of courage," Faye said. "It's finding the key, the way you found the key for me. You said a man had let me fall so only a man could restore my confidence, and you were right. Buck needs a key."

"Yes, it's so obvious when you put it like that," Jason said. "But what's Buck's key and how do I find it? I feel I'm letting him down again."

"Perhaps it isn't up to you," Faye said thoughtfully. "You don't know exactly why he's frightened because he can't tell you the way I could."

"But surely it's plain? He was shot. He was in pain."

"Hadn't he ever been hurt before?"

"Well, yes but—" Jason stopped and stared at her. "What are you saying, Faye?"

"I'm not quite sure. But this was more than physical pain, wasn't it? It was betrayal."

"But he couldn't have known."

"Why not? Dogs are sensitive to atmosphere. When did you know you'd been betrayed?"

"When I saw that gun pointing straight at me, no— before that. Almost as soon as it started I felt it. *Yes....*"

"If you knew, he knew," Faye said. "That's what's really scared him."

"Of course," Jason groaned. "He'd been raised to work as part of a team, and the members of a team have to trust each other implicitly. Betrayal is the worst crime there is. And I thought I was dealing with physical fear. But how does this help me to know what to do for him?"

"You can't. It'll happen when he's ready."

"Or maybe he never will be ready," Jason said somberly. "I dreamed of us working together. He would have been the ideal partner for a private detective."

"What will you do if he can't overcome his fear? Jason." She clutched his arm. "You wouldn't have him put down?"

"Of course not. I'd keep him as a pet. But it won't be the same, and he'll hate it. He's been trained to work and he needs to do that work to be happy."

"Just like you," she said softly.

"And like you, if it comes to that." He reddened slightly and said, "I seem to remember once saying you'd never done a job that you loved, so you wouldn't understand the feeling of exile when you were shut out of it. You shouldn't have let me talk that kind of nonsense."

"We didn't know each other then," she said. "And you thought everything bad about me. If I'd told you I wanted to be a dancer again, you wouldn't have believed me."

"How could I? Nothing about you is the way it seems, that's what's confused me from the start." He kissed her tenderly. "But I should have followed my instincts. In my heart I couldn't accept that you really intended to marry Niall. Now I know you're just playing him along until your father's better." He seized her in his arms. "You'll marry me, won't you? You *must* marry me because I can't do without you."

Faye's eyes shone as she looked up at his face. "I can't think of anything I want more in life than to marry you, Jason."

"Except dancing?"

"No, I want you more than that," she said softly, and found herself crushed in a bear hug. She was nearly a foot shorter and he had to lean down to brush his lips against her hair.

"Darling, are you sure?" he asked. "I don't have any money."

"That's all right. Neither do I."

"I don't even have a proper living. Being a private detective isn't most people's idea of security."

"Who wants security? I wouldn't know what to do with it. I've lived out of a trunk since I was sixteen. Besides, once I start going to auditions again I'll soon get work." Her smile faded and she said softly, "Just love me, Jason. That's all I ask."

He pulled her against him again, leaning down to kiss her hungrily and she gave in to the kiss, pervaded by a happiness so great that her heart almost stopped from the intensity of it. When they pulled apart she discovered, to her amazement, that they were in a downpour.

"It began to rain and we never noticed," Jason said, grinning.

She laughed with him. "We'd better get back."

It took them a while to find Buck and while they were hunting the summer storm increased, so that despite the protection from the trees they were soaked through by the time they got back to the pavilion. Faye hurried into the bathroom, got the biggest bath towel she could find and tossed it over Buck. "Poor old boy," she murmured as she rubbed him down. "We mustn't let you get cold."

"What about me?" Jason demanded.

"There's another towel in the bathroom."

"Thanks!" he said indignantly. "He gets the five-star treatment; I'm told to shift for myself."

She made a face at him. "I can't abide jealous men."

"In that case I'll keep quiet and slip away." He went into the bathroom and a few moments later Faye heard the sound of water in the shower.

She finished with Buck and went into the bathroom, pulling off her clothes. A moment later she was in the shower with Jason. He stopped soaping himself long enough to pull her against him, then continued, lathering her back. She shivered with pleasure as his strong hands slithered over her, tracing the length of her spine and cupping her buttocks. She pressed closer to him, feeling his manhood rampant, throbbing against her flesh, and wild fantasies possessed her at the thought of the loving to come.

"Now the other way." He turned her around and soaped her front, curving his hands around her breasts and teasing the nipples as he went. She gasped at the series of shocks that went through her at every provocative movement of his fingers. The slippery soap added an extra dimension to the action, especially when he flattened his hands against her and let them slide slowly, sensuously down her front to the top of her legs, then back over her hips, caressing her firm flesh luxuriously.

"Mmm," she said blissfully, and slid around in the circle of his arms to face him. She began to wash his chest hair, making whorls with her fingers that crept closer and closer to the nipples while his face grew more taut and his manhood grew harder and more demanding.

"Rinse?" she asked, reaching for the tap.

He grinned. "Yes, but don't make it too cold. I'd hate to spoil it."

She turned on the spray and Jason dropped his head to touch her lips with his own while water cascaded over them. When they'd finished showering he put on a terry-cloth bathrobe and wrapped a huge towel around her before picking her up and walking to the bedroom to sit down on the edge of the bed with her on his lap. "You're so tiny," he said. "You vanish in my arms. Now what's funny?" She had looked up at him with a provocative, mischievous smile.

"Tiny, am I?" she teased. "I can give as good as I get."

"You certainly can," he said in a voice of profound satisfaction.

"If I could just get my arms free..." she said, making a play of struggling against him.

Jason immediately tightened his own arms around her, but not so firmly that she couldn't move. "Think you can escape me, huh?" he demanded.

She wriggled harder. He countered by dropping back onto the bed and holding her against him, and they wrestled for a couple of minutes, by which time they were both more or less dry. Jason looked down at her lying in his arms and the laughter faded from his face. Slowly he pulled the towel away from her. She was soft and sweet smelling, and he began to trail his hand lovingly across her pale skin. "Each time I see you I wonder at how beautiful you are," he whispered. "I keep expecting to discover that my memory is wrong, because no one could be so lovely. But then I see you again and find I didn't do you justice. How can any woman be so perfect?"

"Just two arms and legs," she teased, although it was getting harder to breathe as her excitement rose.

Jason smiled, teasing her in his turn. "Don't forget the bit that joins them all together," he said. "It's rather special." As he spoke he ran his fingertips gently over her throat down to the meeting of her legs and back again, coming to rest over a breast that was yearning for his touch. "All my favorite places," he said huskily.

Shock waves ran through Faye at the agonizingly sweet feel of his hand on her flesh. This glorious union was what she waited for from the first moment she awoke every morning. It haunted her dreams by night and her thoughts by day and she began to look forward to the next loving as soon as the last one was ended. At the thought of becoming one with Jason now she felt her inside turn to molten liquid and her skin begin to burn. Only a short time ago she hadn't even known of this man's existence. Now her love for him was her reason for living; it was why the sun rose and set. It was why her heart beat.

Though their time as lovers had been brief, they'd learned quickly about each other. Their passion seemed to have reached a miraculous stage where they enjoyed the best of both worlds, the confidence of experience as well as the excitement of discovery. It was a devastating combination and they were ready to relish it to the full.

Behind a seemingly relaxed manner Jason's eyes were alert, watching for the little signs that would tell him he was pleasing her, while his body ached for the caresses she knew how to give. He'd discovered that she made love like a dancer, with a delicate strength and suppleness that no ordinary woman could have matched, and which excited him unbearably. She had a thousand little movements, known only to herself, by which she drove him on, lashing his desire to greater heights with her own. He'd thought he knew the confusingly different facets of her personality, but when she lay in his arms he discovered there were yet more.

And then the thoughts would dissolve into darkness and heat, the musky odor of arousal and need, the sounds of sighing, soft with longing at first, then harsh with urgency. There was a light on her face as she took him into her body, though whether it was of rapture or triumph he couldn't tell. He only knew that the perfect union of their flesh was no accident, but the working out of something predestined. The moans that broke from her throat as he drove into her incited him to claim her more deeply, and he was rewarded by her explosive response. As she had said, she could give as good as she got, and she met every thrust with a surge toward him as though she were trying to deny their separateness.

But it couldn't be denied forever. At last the glory began to fade and they became two people again. As he left her Jason thought he saw a wild look in her eyes that might almost have been despair, but he couldn't be sure, because she buried her face against him, clinging to him until her shudders passed and her body calmed. When he next looked into her face she was smiling, and he reproved himself for being fanciful.

Chapter Eleven

Faye was coming downstairs when the phone rang. Jason answered it and she heard a curt note come into his voice almost immediately. When he turned to look at her he was frowning. "It's your friend Luther."

Faye took the receiver from him and spoke into it warmly. She wanted Jason to know that she wasn't turning against her friends just because of his irrational suspicions. "It's lovely to hear from you," she said.

"Bless you, love. Look, you couldn't pop into town for a little chin-wag, could you?"

"That's a splendid idea. I haven't seen you alone for a gossip yet."

"Yeah, that's just it. Talk about the old times, eh? But just you. Not that Jason bloke. We can't natter with him around, and he gives me the willies."

"You leave him to me," Faye said, glancing at Jason who was propped against the wall, arms folded, regarding her sardonically.

"There's a pizza place on the corner of Elvin Street. See you there in an hour?"

"I'll be there." She hung up and turned to confront Jason. His expression made it plain he was going to be unreasonable.

"Leave him to you?" he echoed. "You wouldn't be talking about me by any chance?"

"I would," she said, slipping him a kiss, which he received with pleasure. "I'm going to have a snack with Luther and I don't need a chaperon, thank you."

"What you want and what you're going to get are two different things," he retorted, returning the kiss. "You don't go out of this house without me."

"Come on, darling, it's Luther, a dear old friend."

"Not for Luther or anyone else."

"But we want to talk privately."

"Then I'll sit a discreet distance away, keeping you in sight but out of earshot. That's my best offer. Take it or leave it."

"And suppose I don't want to take it?" she demanded quizzically.

He had her up against the wall, one hand on either side of her head. She met his eyes, enjoying the feel of his body pressing gently against hers, and enjoying even more the half smile that played at his mouth. If only she hadn't promised to go out, she thought longingly. She knew just how to play on that smile and bring a look of heated longing into his eyes, and then they would slip away together....

"Either I go with you, or you don't go," Jason told her implacably. His voice softened. "Come to think of it, that's a good idea."

"Mm, it's a wonderful idea," she said breathlessly.

"Call him back and say you're not coming."

For a brief moment she was tempted, but then she realized she couldn't be so unkind to Luther. "Get thee behind me, Satan," she whispered.

With one swift movement Jason pulled her away from the wall and swung her around until he was behind her. Then he crossed his arms over her breasts and held her against him. "Like this, do you mean?" he whispered in her ear.

"No, not like that," she said, trying to maintain some control. "Don't kiss my neck that way. It isn't fair."

"So who wants to be fair?" he demanded, doubling his efforts.

"I know what you're trying to do...."

"Uh-uh! I'm trying to make you want to stay here with me." She felt his chuckle against her neck. "And I'm succeeding, aren't I?"

"Yes, you are," she gasped as the sweet familiar fire scorched through her. "Oh, Jason..."

"Let's go to the pavilion," he pleaded.

"No," she said as firmly as she could. "I promised. Please, darling, let me go."

"Do you really want me to let you go?"

"You know the answer to that. But please..."

With a reluctant sigh he did so. "We go into town then."

She didn't argue anymore, knowing it would be useless. And she didn't really want to let Jason out of her sight. She looked in on Alaric to tell him where she was going, then hurried out to where Jason was waiting for her with the car. He drove her into town and found Elvin Street without any trouble.

Luther was already there, sitting at a table in a shadowy corner. He looked up and his face fell when he saw Jason. Jason appeared not to notice. He greeted Luther with bland courtesy before moving off to another table. He seated himself so that he was between Faye and the street entrance, with a clear view of the only other door that led to the kitchens. His right arm was clear of the wall and ready for immediate action. Observing these careful preparations Faye felt a twinge of apprehension as she thought of the day that couldn't be delayed much longer, the day when she must tell him everything.

"I thought it was going to be just us," Luther said.

"So did I, but...Jason felt he ought to come, too," Faye said evasively.

Luther regarded her shrewdly. "He's your minder, ain't he?"

"In a manner of speaking. But he's out of earshot. He won't trouble us."

"He troubles me just by being there," Luther confessed. "It ain't easy to say what I've got to, and with him there..."

"Forget him. Tell me what's the matter. You sound so serious."

"Yeah, well, when a feller can't pay his rent, that's serious," he said with an awkward little laugh.

"Oh, no. Luther I'm sorry. I should have realized you might be in trouble."

"Nah, why should you? When you knew me before I was always living high off the hog. Too high. That was my trouble. I never put any aside for a rainy

day. Only now it's raining crocodiles.'' He gave her his
old perky grin as he made the joke against himself and
she took his hand. He squeezed hers convulsively and
didn't say anything for a moment. Then he called the
waiter to order her a pizza, but Faye stopped him. ''I
can afford a pizza,'' he assured her, adding, ''if it's a
small one.''

''I'm not hungry,'' she insisted.

''Have a glass of the house red with me then. It's
horrible but have it anyway.''

She accepted one for the sake of his pride. ''Faye,''
he said quickly, ''it half kills me to be a beggar
but—''

''Of course,'' she said, opening her purse before he
could say anymore.

''It's just until my luck turns. I'll pay you back,
honest.''

''Of course you will. But no hurry.''

The bills she took out were almost the last she had
but she couldn't explain that. To Luther she was the
fiancée of a millionaire, and it broke her heart to see
him down on his luck. He took the money and pock-
eted it without looking at her and his words of thanks
were an inaudible mumble. But she wasn't offended.
She'd seen the tears in his eyes. ''Isn't there anything
else you can do?'' she asked him sympathetically.

''The only thing I know is dancing and I can't do
much of that anymore. I've got arthritis. It takes me
half the day to get moving. I won't kid you, Faye. I've
been a bad lad. Booze and horses. That's where the
money went . . . well, most of it. I squandered a bit on
wild women, but on the whole I fancied females best
when they had four legs and were galloping past the
winning post.''

"Well, I knew that," she said. "You took me to the racetrack with you once, and taught me how to bet. Remember?"

"S'trewth, so I did. And you listened to me very seriously, then bet on some no-hoper because it was called Carmen. You said it would be lucky."

"And you gave me a lecture about how unscientific methods never worked . . ."

"And it romped home at ten to one. You made a packet. It took me a long time to forgive you for that." They laughed together. Then Luther said in a puzzled way, "It's a funny thing. Horses don't seem to run fast when they know I'm backing them. They're all right at other times, though."

She smiled at his droll expression. Luther's humor had to find an outlet, even at his own expense.

"You won't forget me when you're hitched to your rich feller, will you, love?" he asked suddenly.

"I'll never forget you, Luther."

"Yeah, but—you know what I mean."

She did know, and it was almost unbearably painful to feel that she was his last hope and that he was going to be disappointed. She took his hand. "Wherever I am, whatever I'm doing, I'm always your friend and you can always come to me for help," she said simply.

He squeezed her hand and they sat in companionable silence until she said, "I ought to be getting back."

"Sure. Keep in touch, love."

"I will," she promised.

On the way home Jason said, "So he wanted a handout."

"Let's not talk about him, Jason. We'll never see eye to eye about Luther and I don't want to quarrel."

"Would you quarrel with me about him?" he asked mildly.

"Well, I'm funny that way," she retorted. "I don't like hearing my friends slandered. So let's drop it."

"Fine."

Out of sight of the house he stopped the car and pulled her against him for a long, purposeful kiss. "That's to keep me going until the next time," he said breathlessly when they'd finished. "Now let's go inside and try to look sedate."

They went in to see Alaric, who was just waking from his nap. In answer to his questions Faye told him how she'd spent the afternoon. "Poor Luther," he sighed with easy sympathy. "It must be a terrible life being a dancer, all uncertainty and no security."

"That's not what you said when I wanted to dance," Faye reminded him. "You said you were glad I had the courage to risk everything for glory."

"I was carried away by your enthusiasm, darling," he answered quickly. "But we were both wrong, as your accident proved. I'm glad you've discovered the value of security. It's the one thing that never fails."

He reached for her left hand as though to touch her ring for luck, but stopped suddenly. "Your engagement ring—where is it?"

"I took it off," Faye said, laughing awkwardly. "It's too valuable to wear all the time. It might get lost."

He turned anxious eyes on her. "Everything's all right, isn't it? You and Conroy haven't quarreled?"

"Dad, please don't upset yourself...."

"Of course I get upset . . . you mustn't do anything silly, Faye . . ."

"I'm not going to do anything silly. I've still got the ring, I promise."

"Then you should wear it," he insisted. "That's what an engagement ring is for, to show the world that you've made a promise and you mean to keep it."

"All right, I'll put it on again tonight."

Jason watched, frowning, wondering how Alaric, who loved his daughter, could so willfully blind himself to her true needs. He thought he was beginning to understand something of her problem. It gave him an uneasy feeling when he saw the ring on her finger again that evening, but he tried not to let his displeasure show.

The following morning, when Buck's training session was over, the two of them went for a stroll. On his way around the house Jason looked up longingly to the top floor where he knew Faye would be doing bar practice. He would have loved to go up there and surprise her, see the concentration in her face dissolve into joy at the sight of him. But Faye's practice time was sacred and he knew better than to disturb her.

They wandered into the little wood and rambled contentedly for half an hour. Buck explored rabbit holes but without result. "I guess someone warned them you were coming," Jason commiserated with him.

"I beg your pardon."

Jason looked around and saw Alaric standing there. "I thought I was alone here," Alaric said. "You gave me the fright of my life."

Despite his words he looked fit and cheery. But Jason asked, "Where's your nurse?"

"I gave Don the morning off. Sometimes it's nice to be mollycoddled and sometimes it's nice to take a walk in a wood by myself."

"I thought you despised nature," Jason reminded him with a grin. "Concrete over the country, you said."

"I say a lot of things," Alaric riposted. "They aren't necessarily an indication of what I'm thinking. It's true that I've never been a nature lover, but the world looks different to me since I nearly left it. And this is a pretty time of year."

"Just the same, why don't we drift back to the house?" Jason urged, and Alaric laughed and let himself be led away.

Faye wasn't down yet, so they settled into two reclining chairs on the terrace. Now Jason could see that Alaric looked more tired and drawn than he'd seemed in the mellow light of the wood. "It was about time you came back," he observed.

"Yes, I'm rather apt to overdo things now that I feel my strength returning," Alaric admitted. "But I'm determined to be really well for Faye's wedding."

"I know she won't marry until she's easy in her mind about you," Jason said carefully.

"The sooner she marries the better. She's always worked hard, poor dear. I shall enjoy seeing her take it easy."

"There's a little more to marriage than that," Jason said. "You know the kind of man Niall is. You don't really think she's in love with him, do you?"

"He's in love with her," Alaric said firmly. "That's the thing that really matters. She'll be pampered as no other woman has ever been."

Jason found this refusal to face facts so outrageous that he couldn't keep an edge out of his voice as he replied, "Putting aside the question of whether Niall is capable of being in love as most people would understand it, Faye doesn't strike me as the kind of woman who wants pampering. I think she prefers to be independent."

There was a perceptible chill in the air as Alaric replied, "I don't mean to be impolite, Jason, but you're hardly in a position to know what my daughter wants or needs. Your impression of her in this place has been a very superficial one. But she and Conroy got to know each other when she thought I was dying. At times like that people's real selves come to the surface. She...came to admire his strength and—and lean on him."

You can't really believe such a fairy tale, Jason thought, dismayed. Cautiously he persisted, "But surely she needs more than that? She won't be happy if she marries a man she doesn't love."

"What do you mean by love?" Alaric asked vaguely. "There are so many different kinds and each person knows which kind suits them. I find that if you leave things alone they usually work out for the best."

There was a note of finality in his voice, and he stretched out in his seat with his eyes closed. Jason sighed and gave up. It had been like trying to talk to a man who'd pulled up a drawbridge. Alaric simply didn't want to listen.

Faye adores you, he thought, looking at him. *So there has to be more to you than there seems. I just wish I knew what it was.*

He stayed there, brooding over the puzzle, and gradually he became aware that his companion had dozed off. His breathing was slower and he began to mutter disjointed words.

"I had to do it . . . had to do it . . ." Alaric was saying jerkily. "You don't know . . . had to do it . . . had to do it . . ."

He was sounding more distressed with every second. Jason reached over to awake him, but before he could do so Alaric gave a little scream and began to gabble, "Not prison . . . I can't go to prison . . . pay it back . . . not prison . . . please, Mr. Niall."

Frowning, Jason squeezed his arm gently. Alaric jerked out of sleep and shot halfway up in his chair. His eyes were wide and staring and tremors racked his body. "It's all right," Jason soothed. "You're awake now. Do you want me to fetch Faye?"

"No," Alaric said hurriedly. "It was just a bad dream, nothing more."

"But a pretty realistic-sounding dream," Jason said. "You were asking Niall not to send you to prison."

Alaric made a valiant effort to pull himself together. "Well, sometimes—dreams—you know . . ." He gave up and slumped back in his chair. "Oh, God."

"Why don't you tell me? What has Niall got on you?"

Alaric's voice was full of defeat. "I forged his name on a check. He found out."

"And threatened you with jail?"

"Yes," Alaric admitted.

Jason stared. "Is that why Faye became engaged to him?"

"Of course not. She—that is—" He sighed wearily. "I don't know. She says not, but I don't know."

To his relief Jason saw Don coming around the side of the house, still in outdoor clothes from his morning off. "Take care of him," he said to the nurse, and hurried into the house.

He went first to the gymnasium but Faye wasn't there. Next he tried her room, and as soon as he went inside he heard sounds coming from the shower. He looked into the bathroom and saw her dimly through the frosted glass of the shower screen. As he stood there she switched the water off and pushed back the screen, smiling when she saw him. For a moment the sight of her beautiful nakedness, streaming with water, almost drove everything else from his mind, and he drew her toward him. But after kissing her briefly he let her go. There were things he had to know.

"What is it, darling?" Faye asked as she tied the bathrobe around herself. "Is something wrong?"

"Not wrong exactly, just puzzling. Faye, why didn't you tell me the real reason you became engaged to Niall?"

He didn't know how he'd expected her to look, but he wasn't prepared for the uneasy expression that flickered across her face. For reasons that he didn't want to face it worried him. "I've been talking to your father," he said. "He says Niall has something on him, threatened to send him to jail. Is that right?"

"Yes." Out of sight Faye crossed her fingers, knowing that the moment had come.

"So why didn't you tell me?" Jason demanded. "I don't mean in the beginning, but when we knew we loved each other... surely I had the right to know?"

"You have the right to know everything, Jason. It's just that it isn't easy to tell you. Dad did it because he wanted to take better care of me when I was injured.

Conroy found out and bullied him until he had that heart attack, and he still has the evidence. Conroy said he'd give it to me when we were engaged, but of course he didn't."

"You mean he's blackmailing you?"

"Do you think I'd have looked at him for a second otherwise? Now he says I can have the evidence when we're married, but I think he'll go on holding it over my head—"

"Of course he would, *if* you married him," Jason agreed. "But you're going to marry *me*. So we have to get it away from him."

Her heart lifted. "You say that so easily. *Can* you make him give it up?"

"I can handle Niall," he assured her grimly. "He's not a brave man and I can be very persuasive. You'll be free of him for good. I promise you."

"Oh, thank God!" she burst out, overwhelmed with relief. She pressed her hands to her mouth, afraid that she was going to break down at the sudden easing of her burdens.

"Hey, come on," he said, taking hold of her. "Trust me, Okay?"

"I do," she said, leaning against him. "It's just so wonderful not to be alone anymore." She was talking fast, words falling over each other in her eagerness. "I couldn't see any way out and I dreaded having to marry him, but then I met you and it was like an answer to my prayers. But sometimes you seemed to hate me and I was so frightened—"

The world seemed to stop for him. In that terrible inner silence he relived all the memories that troubled him: the time he'd spoken of the kidnap attempt and she hadn't known for a moment what he was talking about; the evening in the nightclub when he'd confided in her, only to discover that she knew everything already from a computer; the way she'd always shrugged off his fears for her safety—*like a woman who knew there was nothing to fear.*

He tried to tell himself that he was overreacting but suddenly it all pointed to a conclusion too monstrous to be true. "Scared of what, Faye?" he asked quietly. "Scared that you couldn't make me fall in love with you?"

She looked up. "Jason—"

Jason spoke in a strange voice, like a man contemplating a nightmare. "Just how long ago did you cast me in the role of your rescuer? You thought of it a lot sooner than I did, didn't you?"

He released her and moved away. He didn't seem angry, just quiet and puzzled, but Faye wasn't fooled. This was life or death for them both. "I thought of it as soon as I saw you," she admitted, knowing she had to speak the truth for both their sakes—but it was hard.

"That would be the night I drove the two of you home?"

"Yes."

"And then you went indoors with Niall and got him to call up my file on his computer so that you could make sure my qualifications were satisfactory?"

"I asked Conroy who you were and he called up the file. But I didn't need that. When I saw you I just knew. Jason, I know it sounds bad but if you understood how desperate I was—desperate enough to do something I would never dream of doing normally."

He stopped pacing and faced her. His face revealed nothing, but the distance he kept between them told Faye the worst. "And then, by a remarkable coincidence, someone tried to kidnap you?"

She shook her head, her eyes fixed on his face.

"There was no kidnap attempt?"

"No. I needed time to get to know you, and that was all I could think of."

"You invented the whole story so that Niall would hire me to protect you, preferably here where it's nice and secluded and you'd have me to yourself? Am I about right so far?"

"Yes, but—"

"No, let me finish. I'm really lost in admiration for the way you managed to make a fool of Niall and me at the same time. You even got him to pay my salary while you set about seducing me so that I'd turn on him. That took some work. I've met connivers before but you take the gold medal.

"Not that I gave you much trouble, did I? You know how to make a man fall for you, and the rest was easy." There was bitter scorn in his voice but it was directed at himself. "I fell into your trap like a green boy. And here's the joke—I started off suspicious. I knew the first day that something about you wasn't right. I've learned to listen to my instincts, and they warned me loud and clear, but I ignored them."

"Jason, please listen. I hated doing it, but I was frantic. I couldn't bear to marry Conroy, but I had to save my father, too. I did everything I could to find another way. You were my last chance. Why won't you try to understand?"

He looked at her with disillusioned eyes. "Because you *deceived* me, and deception is the one thing I can't take. You know why. I loved you. I believed in you. I thought you loved me, but all the time you were planning to use me."

"If that were all, I could have told you the truth days ago. Why do you think I didn't? Because I fell in love with you, and I knew the truth might destroy the relationship. It seemed so easy at first. Yes, I planned to get you on my side and I know that sounds calculating. But I made that plan before I knew you. When I discovered the kind of man you are it became hard to tell you. I've been racking my brains for a way to do it without hurting you, without hurting us."

He'd been pacing the room but at these last words he turned on her. "Save it, Faye," he snapped. "We're past that now. I've started remembering things, like the way you sought me out in the first days. That day in the gym you went for me with guns blazing and I was actually flattered. More fool me! And the night we went out, and you let me think I was forcing my company on you. I did exactly what you'd always meant me to do, didn't I?"

"Jason—"

"Didn't I, Faye?"

"Yes," she admitted unhappily. "I've deceived you, I can't deny it. My only excuse is that at the time it felt as though anything would be justifiable to escape Conroy. And then I fell in love with you. I know you find that hard to believe, but it's true."

"You're wrong, Faye. I don't find it hard to believe. I find it impossible to believe. And you should have known better than to try that line on me now. But you were bound to, weren't you? Because deceit and seduction are all you know. I wish I'd never met you, and I hope to God I can manage to forget you quickly."

Ignoring her restraining hand he left the room and she heard him hurrying down the stairs. Frantically she began to dress, but before she'd finished she heard the sound of the car. She looked out the window just in time to see it vanish down the driveway.

Chapter Twelve

Conroy's secretary looked up at Jason, whom she recognized, and asked, "Is he expecting you?"

"No, but he's going to see me. Is he alone?"

"For the moment, but he has a string of appointments—"

"They can wait. I'm going in."

The receptionist flicked a switch. "Mr. Royce says he must see you urgently," she paraphrased diplomatically. Jason had pushed open the door of Conroy's office before she finished speaking.

Conroy was on his feet. He looked up when he heard the door and demanded sharply, "Why aren't you with Faye? Has something happened?"

"Nothing's happened and nothing's going to."

"Then how dare you leave your post—"

"Shut up and listen. I'm here because I have things to say to you, and after that we won't meet again."

'You must be mad to talk to me like this.''

Jason gave an unpleasant laugh. "I was mad when I came to work for you, and the woman who's as scheming and crooked as you are. But now I'm sane again and I'm going back to where I can breathe clean air, back where it's easier to tell who's a friend and who is an enemy.''

"I've heard enough of this nonsense," Conroy snapped, touching his intercom. But before he could speak Jason placed a large hand over the machine, cutting it off. He gave Conroy a chilling smile and, still smiling, ripped the cord from the wall. Then he did the same with the telephone, walked back to the door and locked it. "Now we can talk without being disturbed," he said. "Sit down."

Conroy found his voice. "If you think you can—"

"Sit down."

Conroy obeyed, scowling but not otherwise troubled, clearly confident that his wealth and power were such that he had nothing to fear. Then he looked up at Jason looming over him, and knew a moment of doubt.

"The sooner you cooperate the sooner you'll be rid of me," Jason observed.

"What do you mean, 'cooperate'?"

"I mean hand over everything you have on Alaric Stafford."

Conroy's face set in hard lines. "I don't know what you're talking about," he snapped.

The words were hardly out before his head was pushed back by a hand at his throat, and Jason's face, livid with hate, was close to his. "Don't waste my time," he said softly and emphatically. He released

Conroy and waited until the other man had stopped making choking noises.

"I don't know what Faye's told you," Conroy said hoarsely, "but you ought to know that she's mentally unbalanced, totally unreliable. You'd be stupid to believe a word she says."

"But I do believe it," Jason declared flatly. "I know you blackmailed her because nothing else would explain her agreeing to marry a dirty little toe rag like you."

"Nothing else except my money," Conroy choked. "Surely you've known enough women to spot a gold digger when you see one?"

"I thought I did," Jason said, half to himself.

"Then for God's sake open your eyes and see what's happening now. I won't bother to ask what's been going on while my back was turned, because it's obvious. But now that she's had her fun, you're an inconvenience. I suppose you begged her to go away with you and live on love, and she invented this tale to explain why she was going to stick with me. She didn't reckon on your getting an attack of knight-errantry and coming to see me. Take my word for it, no matter what she's told you, Faye is marrying me of her own free will."

"It was her father who first told me what had happened."

For a moment Conroy was shaken, but he recovered and gave a nervous laugh. "Of course, they're in it together. You've been taken for the biggest ride of your life, bigger even than what Wainright did to you. But some men never learn."

Jason said nothing, but looked thoughtful. Emboldened, Conroy went on, "You should be grateful

I'm a reasonable man. I can understand your losing your head over her. She's very beautiful. I'm even prepared to overlook your leaving her unprotected.''

"She doesn't need any protection," Jason said. "There was no kidnap attempt. She told me so."

Conroy stared. "What the hell are you talking about?"

"She invented the story so that—"

"Well, there you are then," Conroy interrupted with a screech of triumph. "Doesn't that prove what I'm telling you, that she's a compulsive liar?"

Jason nodded slowly, and sat down. "I suppose it does, now that I come to think of it." He seemed troubled.

"I knew you'd see sense." Conroy made a nervous movement, as if to rise, and when Jason didn't try to stop him he got boldly to his feet. "As I said, I'm a reasonable man, and I'm assuming that you are, too. Fooling around with a woman is all very well, but after all, she's only a woman. A man has to think seriously about the future, and that means money. How would you manage with that little gold digger?"

"You seemed ready to take a risk," Jason observed mildly.

"Ah, but I know what I'm getting, and how much I'm prepared to pay for it."

"You mean you'll still marry her, even now?"

"After she's had a roll in the hay with you? Why not? She's beautiful and she belongs to me. I'll settle my accounts with Faye after we're married, and after that she won't give me any more trouble. So you needn't feel any sense of guilt at leaving her. You haven't ruined her future prospects."

"Am I going to leave her?" Jason enquired, the irony in his tone lost on Conroy.

"I think you will when you hear what I have to propose." Conroy approached a modern picture hanging on the wall and pulled it back on a hinge, revealing a safe underneath. Hiding the knob, he opened the safe, reached inside and took out a wad of bank notes with a paper seal around them. "Do you see this?" he asked, holding it out to Jason.

"I see it," Jason said without apparent interest.

"Know how much is here? A thousand pounds. Look at that." He flicked the notes. "A thousand, and it's yours for the asking. No paperwork, no questions asked."

"And you think my price is a thousand pounds?"

"That's just a taster. Look at this." Conroy took out several more wads and laid them on the desk. "Ten thousand," he said, "in fifty-pound notes."

"And what do I do in exchange?" Jason asked.

"You vanish. You forget Faye's silly stories, you don't contact her, and you disappear off the face of the earth. I'll explain everything to her."

Jason shrugged. "No need. She'll guess what happened when I don't come back."

Conroy relaxed perceptibly. "Now you're talking sense at last. I knew we could do business."

"Wait a minute," Jason stopped him. "I didn't say I'd agreed. The idea's all right in principle, but I don't come that cheap."

"You call ten thousand pounds cheap?" Conroy sneered.

"It's cheap to a man with your money. My price is fifty thousand."

After a moment Conroy shrugged. "All right, fifty thousand. Here." He grabbed the notes that were left in the safe and hurled them onto the desk. "It's all yours."

Jason rose in leisurely fashion and fingered through the money, checking the amount. Then he grunted as if satisfied. "All mine, huh?"

"Every last penny."

Jason grinned. "Damned if I ever thought I'd own fifty thousand pounds all at once. And the beauty of it is that I can do whatever I like with it."

"Whatever you like," Conroy echoed.

"And what I'd like to do with it—is this."

Moving so casually that Conroy didn't realize what was happening Jason took up the heavy lighter from the desk, flicked it open and held a wad of notes in the flame. When it was half burned he tossed it into Conroy's steel waste bin, and took up another one. "What the hell do you think you're doing?" Conroy screamed.

He grabbed for the money but Jason snatched him like a mad dog and held him off with a viselike grip on his collar. Conroy's toes barely touched the floor as he choked from Jason's hold on him and the acrid smoke that was efficiently sucked away by the air vents. He twisted and flailed, trying impotently to escape Jason, while the rest of the money went up in smoke. A moan broke from Conroy's throat.

When it was over Jason released him. Conroy dropped to his knees and began to scrabble among the ashes, vainly seeking a note that was in one piece. "You animal," he sobbed. "I'll have the law on you."

"What for? Burning my own money?"

"You're insane."

"You'd think so. Now get up." He jerked Conroy to his feet. "You can cry over your murdered babies later. Right now I want what I asked for—everything you have on Alaric Stafford."

"You're mad," Conroy choked. "I've bought you off."

Jason gave a wolfish grin. "I don't remember."

"We had a deal—fifty thousand pounds—"

"I don't see any fifty thousand pounds, do you?" Conroy's only answer was a snarl of rage. "Now get me what I came here for. I'm running out of patience."

"You saw inside the safe. There was nothing else there."

"You wouldn't keep this in your office safe. You'd have a special place for it. *Get it*, unless you want me to break your neck." He took a menacing step forward.

Looking into his burning eyes, Conroy believed he meant it. "All right," he said in a shaky voice. "Let me go."

"No. Direct me to it."

"It's part of the desk—there's a special spring— you'll never find it."

Jason released him and followed him over to the desk, watching that he didn't move out of line. But he needn't have bothered. The burning of the money had demoralized Conroy as nothing else could have, and there was no fight left in him. He opened a drawer of the steel desk, fumbled inside and found the catch that opened an inner drawer. From it he took an envelope. "Take it and get out," he said, looking at his tormentor with hate.

"When I've checked the contents," Jason said, tipping papers into his hand.

"Everything's there," Conroy insisted sullenly. "There's the actual check, presented at a bank account that turned out to be Alaric Stafford's. Some of the other sheets are memos from various staff members about procedures in the financial department. When they're all put together they narrow it down to him. The last one is a signed confession in his own handwriting."

"Very thorough," Jason remarked, casting his eyes over the papers. Suddenly he looked up. "And the rest," he said.

"What rest?"

"The *rest*. The thing you kept back on its own in case this day ever came. You see, I know how your mind works. Somewhere you've got one last damning paper hidden away, and I want it. You have five seconds. One...two..."

"All right, all right. Here," Conroy almost screamed as he unlocked a small flap in the thick steel of the desk and withdrew another envelope.

Jason examined the contents and grinned without warmth. "A second copy of the confession. You think of everything. But then, so do I."

"You were very sure of yourself," Conroy sneered. "But it was guesswork. Suppose I hadn't been keeping anything back?"

"That would have been your misfortune," Jason said softly, and Conroy blanched.

"I suppose I needn't ask what's going to happen now," Conroy sneered. "You deserve each other. Frankly I think you'll regret the day you ever set eyes on her."

Jason's face was very hard. "Nothing's going to happen. If you want to see if she'll still marry you for love of your money alone, you're free to do so. I just wish I could be a fly on the wall when she gives you her answer." He unlocked the door and walked out.

Conroy stared after him with loathing. His legs were collapsing beneath him and he only just managed to get to his chair. After a moment his secretary appeared in the doorway. "I'm sorry about that, Mr. Niall, but he just—"

"Get out!" Conroy screamed. *"Get out."*

Faye snatched the phone as soon as it rang, hoping it might be Jason. But it was Conroy. "I'm going to make you sorry, Faye," he said with a snarl. "As long as you live you're going to wish you hadn't done it."

"What—I don't understand?"

"Spare me your manufactured innocence. How *dare* you set your boyfriend on me. I suppose you thought you were being very clever, but you'll be sorry you were quite as clever as that." He slammed down the receiver.

Faye stared at the dead telephone, a prey to the ghastliest nightmares. Jason must have gone to see Conroy, but what had happened? Had he recovered the damning evidence? Conroy's threats made it sound as if he hadn't. Now Conroy knew they'd been lovers and was going to take revenge by incriminating Alaric.

She felt herself slipping down into a hell from which only Jason could rescue her. If only he'd come back soon and tell her what had happened. She wondered briefly if his bitterness had made him expose her to Conroy without even trying to recover the evidence, but dismissed that thought as soon as it surfaced. Jason would never be capable of such spite.

They'd had so little time together, but she'd seen his depth. She knew how the generosity of his heart urged him toward love and trust, while his experience pointed him to cynicism and suspicion. Under the tough exterior was a man who could be hurt so easily that he'd armed himself against it. He'd built barricades and told himself he was invulnerable, never seeing the chink through which the right woman could still reach him. And she *was* the right woman for Jason. Her heart told her so with overwhelming certainty. If only Jason could be made to see it, too!

For another two hours she endured wretched uncertainty, but then she was rewarded by the sight of Jason's car coming down the driveway. Her heart leaped and she waited for him at the top of the steps. To her dismay she saw that his face remained cold and unyielding when he saw her. "Come inside," he said curtly.

"Tell me what happened," she begged as they went into the house. "Conroy called, screaming threats that I didn't understand. Did you see him?"

"I saw him. And I got this." Jason pulled out the papers and gave them to her. He watched as she flicked through them eagerly, weeping with relief. "Is everything there?" he demanded.

"It must be. Oh, my God, *two* copies of the confession—and the actual check—I don't understand. How did you get all this?"

"I scared it out of him. He tried to convince me that you'd invented the whole story to get rid of me, and offered me ten thousand pounds to leave quietly."

Jason's voice cracked with hard laughter. "I told him my price was fifty."

"You—what?"

"The only thing he understands is money and, though he's clever, his blind spot is his belief that that is true for everyone. He got the money out of the safe but I set fire to it and forced him to watch it burn to ashes. I don't think anything hurts him as much as losing money without getting anything in return."

"You turned down fifty thousand pounds?" she echoed, glowing. "That was splendid."

"It was sensible. How far do you think I'd have gotten if I'd been fool enough to take it? He'd have called the police the minute I'd left."

"Yes, I suppose so," she said, a little dashed by his indifferent tone. Then she looked again at the papers in her hand and joy swept over her as she realized that the nightmare was over. "He can't touch Dad now. He's safe—safe—" She looked up, her eyes shining. "Thank you," she whispered. "Oh, my darling, thank you."

She was overwhelmed by what had happened. In a moment all her terrors had vanished. Jason had done this for *her*. He'd forgiven her for deceiving him, and now they were free to love each other. She thought her heart would burst with happiness. As emotion flooded her she put her arms around him and laid her mouth against his.

But he didn't move. He stood there stiff in her arms while a chill fell on her heart, and she drew back to search his face. What she saw in it made her freeze. "Jason, don't look at me like that," she pleaded.

"How should I look at you, Faye? Like a dog that's done your bidding and is grateful for a pat?"

"It isn't like that. I love you. And I think you love me, or you wouldn't have done this for me."

"On the contrary. It's because I have no love to give you that I give the only thing in my power—" he pointed at the papers "—the service you hired me for."

"Jason—please, let me—"

He brushed aside her hand as she tried to touch him. "I've done what you wanted, so you don't need to keep on," he said curtly.

She retreated from the scorn in his eyes. "I was trying to thank you," she said.

"Why bother? You paid for my services in advance. And paid handsomely. There's no need for more, even if there was anything I wanted from you."

"*Please*, Jason, try to believe it's not like that. I love you—"

"If I tried for a million years I couldn't believe that you love me, Faye."

"But why should I pretend now, when I've got these?" she cried, holding up the papers.

"I imagine I still have my uses as long as Niall's threatening you. Don't worry. It's me he's angry with. I gave him a hard time."

"I don't believe this is really you talking to me," she said. "I don't believe that what we shared meant so little that you can kill it, even if you try. No." As he turned away she pulled him around to face her. His eyes burned with hate, but there was another flame there, too, one she recognized and answered. "No, I won't let you walk away from me. We belong together. You know we do."

On the last word she pulled his head down and kissed him fiercely, knowing she was fighting for her life. Jason *was* her life, and he mustn't be allowed to leave her.

Jason tried to deaden his senses as he felt her against him, but it was useless. Her mouth was soft and enticing, her slim body carried the memories of loving that had been fierce and tender, burning him with wild passion while bringing his soul an unspeakable peace. But what made his heart almost stop beating was the feel of her tears on his face. He stood there fighting her silently, until at last his arms enclosed her as though of their own will. He groaned as he crushed her helplessly to him, feeling the old fire begin again, melting his insides. He wanted to forget all the bitterness and anger that lay between them and remember only the way she cried out with joy when he made love to her. He wanted to make love to her this minute, love her as never before, and swear that no sacrifice was too much for the beauty she brought him.

But it wasn't true. There was one sacrifice he could never make—his self-respect—which he'd lose if he succumbed to her wiles again. With a mighty effort he found the strength to tear himself from her arms. "No," he said explosively. "Not again. What is it with you? Can't you bear to let your prey escape even now? Must you prove that you can bring the poor fool back to your feet even now? Let me go, Faye. We've come to the end."

"It'll never be at an end for me," she cried. "I'll love you as long as I live, Jason, whether you believe it or not."

"I'd give anything on earth to believe it," he said bleakly. "But tell me honestly, Faye. Do you think I ever could?"

"I could make you," she said passionately.

"Yes, you could make a man believe anything that suited you. But it wouldn't make it true, would it? Now you've got all you ever wanted of me."

She stayed there when he'd left her, trying to sort out her confused reactions of joy and pain. Alaric was free of the fear of jail. She was free of Conroy, free to dance again. Only a little while ago these things were all she had wanted from life. But now they faded beside the fact that the man she loved hated and despised her.

A noise from the hallway made her hurry out to see Jason coming down with his baggage. Buck was behind him. "You're going now?" she asked.

"There's nothing to stay for."

She watched him from the steps as he loaded the bags into the car and opened the back door for Buck. But the dog stopped and looked back at Faye. "Get in," Jason commanded him.

Instead Buck returned to Faye and looked up at her, seemingly puzzled by the hostile atmosphere he could sense. "Buck," Jason called curtly.

Buck looked at him, then back at Faye. He whined and pawed her, seeming to plead. Faye dropped to her knees and put her arms around him, reveling in his thick, silky coat for the last time. "Go with him," she whispered. "Look after him for me."

Slowly Buck walked away from her down the steps. He gave her one last look before he climbed slowly into the car. As it moved down the driveway she could see him looking back at her through the rear window, and he stayed like that until the car disappeared.

Jason drove the few miles to Cranton without allowing himself to think, because that would be dangerous. Buck's reluctance to leave had been hard to bear because it had echoed something in himself. In another moment he, too, would have run back to Faye and sworn that nothing mattered as long as they were together. But he would have despised himself, and in that shadow the long years ahead would have been hideous. He repeated this thought to stop himself from turning the car around.

In Cranton he realized that he was running low on gas and stopped at the first station. As he returned from paying the bill a man came walking by and stopped when he saw him. Jason groaned as he recognized Luther Welbeck.

Luther hailed him and looked in his car. "No Faye?" he asked.

"No," Jason said shortly.

"Off duty, are you?"

"Permanently," Jason snapped, and drove off.

Faye slipped quietly into Alaric's room. She found her father lying in bed, his face flushed and his eyes agitated. She sat on his bed, smiling to cheer him. "I've got some wonderful news," she said. "You don't have to be afraid anymore. Jason saw Conroy and forced him to give back all the evidence against you."

Alaric struggled up in bed. "Let me see." He snatched the papers she gave him and ran through them with feverish hands. "The check, my confession, the second confession."

"You never told me he made you sign two."

"I was too ashamed, darling. He said he was going to keep the other one separately, 'in case of accidents.' How did Jason manage to get that one? He couldn't have known about it.''

"I guess Jason is the kind of man who thinks of everything," Faye said quietly. "He's freed us both. I'm not going to marry Conroy, Dad.''

He looked at her timidly. "That was always the reason, wasn't it, darling?''

"Yes, it was always the reason. But now you're safe I don't have to. I shall try to start as a dancer again.''

Alaric looked back at the papers. "It's all here," he breathed. "He can't do anything to me now. I won't go to jail." Abruptly he burst into tears.

Faye took him in her arms and rocked him back and forth. "It's all right," she said soothingly. "He can't hurt us anymore. But we have to get out of this house, Dad. I want you to get some rest now so that we can go tomorrow.''

"Yes, we'll go home," he said happily. His volatile spirits were already painting the future in rosy colors. "Companies will be falling over themselves to hire you, and I shall write more books. Everything's wonderful again, isn't it, darling?''

"Yes, Dad," she said, glad that he couldn't see her face. "Everything's wonderful.''

She left him to his happy fantasies and went to start packing. She was interrupted by the sound of the phone. She snatched up the receiver, her heart beating with hope in case it was Jason.

But it was only Luther.

"You couldn't pop into town for half an hour, could you, love?" he pleaded. "I'm in a spot of bother.''

"Can't you tell me on the phone?''

"Not really. I need to see you. Please, Faye.''

She didn't want to see anyone while her heart was breaking, but she had to be stronger than that. This was her last chance to see Luther before she left and she still felt she owed him for the help he'd given her in the past. "All right, I'll be there as quickly as I can," she promised.

She looked in on Alaric and found him dozing. As she began to back out of the door he awoke and called, "Is that you, darling?"

"Yes. I'm just going out for a while, Dad. I won't be long."

He waved to her sleepily. She closed the door and hurried away.

Chapter Thirteen

The shrill of the telephone tore Jason from sleep. He groped for it, cursing and rolling over to shift Buck who'd been draped over his feet, snoring noisily. He'd lain awake into the small hours, thinking of Faye, trying not to think of her, increasing his own torment with the effort. At five in the morning he'd dropped into a restless doze, and now it was nearly nine. For a wild moment he hoped the caller might be Faye, then remembered she didn't have his number. "Yes," he growled into the receiver.

It was Detective Inspector Frank Dudley, a police colleague he'd disliked without quite knowing why. Perhaps his ambition was just a little too naked. No policeman could afford to be sentimental, but in Dudley, detachment shaded into callousness, and he seemed content to have it so. "I thought you were supposed to be guarding Conroy Niall's fiancée,'' he said. "You haven't done a very brilliant job."

Jason was instantly alert. "What do you mean?" he demanded.

But he knew. His heart lurched violently inside him even before Dudley said, "She's been kidnapped. They've asked for half a million in ransom."

"They? Who are *they*?" Jason demanded, swinging his legs out of bed as he spoke.

"So far there's nothing definite, just a voice on the phone, demanding money."

"How did they get her?"

"Weren't you supposed to stick with her?"

"How did they get her?" Jason shouted.

"According to her father she took a cab into Cranton yesterday evening and didn't come back. A man phoned to say she'd been kidnapped, and that details of how and where the money should be paid would follow later. Niall wasn't there, so Alaric Stafford tried to call him in London, and this is where it gets strange. He can't get through to Niall anywhere. He's left messages at his home and his office, but Niall doesn't seem bothered enough about his fiancée to ring back."

"That's because she isn't his fiancée anymore," Jason grated. "It's off."

Dudley whistled. "So he's got no reason to ransom her, unless he gets an attack of decency."

"Let's not hold our breath for that."

"I called because I thought you might have a lead. Did anyone try to snatch her while you were with her?"

"No."

"Which is presumably why you felt it was safe to leave your post?"

"You're wasting your time," Jason said curtly. "I have nothing to tell you."

He slammed down the phone before Dudley could pry any further, and sat for a moment with a hand over his eyes. Buck pawed him and whined softly. "You know, don't you?" Jason said. "Even though I didn't say her name, you know it's her."

He didn't wonder how. Buck's intuition was beyond human comprehension, and now he'd recognized a note in his master's voice that was there for only one person in the world.

Jason snatched the phone and dialed the number of Haverill Manor. Martha answered and he asked to speak to Faye's father. After a few moments he heard Alaric's voice. He sounded shaken and older. "Just tell me what happened," Jason instructed him. "Why did Faye go out?"

"I don't know. She just said she was going. She didn't say why."

Jason forced himself to speak calmly. "Did anything happen immediately beforehand?"

"Oh, dear, it's hard to say. I was asleep—at least, not exactly asleep, you know—just dozing, and when you're like that you can't be sure if something really happened or not."

Jason clutched the receiver until his knuckles turned white and with a huge effort wiped the impatience from his voice. "What do you *think* happened?" he asked.

"Well, I may have heard a telephone ringing—or I may have dreamed that. Oh dear, I really can't be sure."

"So if there was a call that's probably why she went out. All right, Alaric, don't worry about it. We'll get Faye back safely."

He was trying to reassure Alaric for the sake of the old man's heart but inside him he had no certainty, only black fear.

He threw on his clothes and in a few minutes he and Buck were in the car heading out of London. He broke the speed limit all the way to Cranton, and when he reached the town he headed straight for the theater. He was sure Alaric hadn't dreamed that phone call, and equally sure he knew who'd made it.

He put his head into the Stage Doorkeeper's cubbyhole and asked, "Is Luther Welbeck here?"

"No, and he should be. He's due for rehearsal this morning but—"

"Where does he live?"

"I'm not allowed to give out that kind of—" the man hesitated at the sight of the ten-pound note Jason held out to him, then resumed "—but I'm sure it'll be all right just once."

He scribbled down the address of a boarding house. Jason thanked him and departed. He found the place without trouble. It was run-down and seedy, with windows that urgently needed cleaning. He rang the doorbell and a slatternly woman put her head out of the upstairs window. "Yes?" she demanded forbiddingly.

"I'm looking for Luther Welbeck," Jason called up.

"Well 'e ain't 'ere."

"Do you know where he is?"

"Nope."

"When did he go?"

"Dunno."

"When will he be back?"

"Dunno." She slammed the window shut.

Jason swore. It was clear that Luther had somehow persuaded the woman not to give him away, and that only increased Jason's conviction that he was on the right track.

"'Ere, mister!" Jason turned and saw a grubby boy of about ten regarding him with interest. "You a debt collector?" the urchin asked.

"No." he said.

"You look like one."

"Have you seen a lot of debt collectors?"

"Yeah. Ever since 'e came. Mom says she's gettin' fed up with it."

"Was that your mother I just talked to?"

"Yeah! She won't ever tell on 'im to debt collectors, 'cos she says if 'e's got anything she's gonna 'ave it for the rent."

"So he's behind with his rent?"

"I'll say. Mom says I can't have the new game I want until he coughs up."

"That's a scandal," Jason said sympathetically. "Any special game?"

"Yeah, Space Monsters."

"How much?"

"Tenner."

Jason produced the money but held it out of reach of the boy's eager grasp. "Where is he?"

"The Three Crows. He always goes to drink there when 'e's 'iding. It's just down there on the left."

Jason handed over the money and hurried back to the car. He found The Three Crows a few hundred yards down, and scouted around it before going in. It was a small pub with only one front entrance and, he guessed, only one at the rear. After leaving Buck in position he walked through the front door.

He spotted Luther at once. At the same moment the sharp-faced little man turned and saw him. He blanched visibly and said something to the bartender, who nodded and lifted the bar flap for Luther to get through. Jason made no move to follow, but departed again through the front door. A deep growl from the alley at the rear told him that his partner was playing his part, and when he went to investigate he found Luther backed up against the wall being treated to a grandstand view of Buck's impressive fangs.

"Get him off me," Luther yelped.

"He isn't on you," Jason observed mildly. "If he were, you'd really know it. I'm afraid Buck doesn't like you. He knows Faye's in danger and he suspects you're responsible. If I told him the part you actually played you'd never get up again. He's very loyal to his friends—unlike you."

"I couldn't help it," Luther sobbed.

"I'm afraid Buck doesn't find that a satisfactory explanation. Neither do I. You'd better tell us more."

"There were these two blokes—I don't know who they were, but they'd been following her. That night you brought Faye to the show, they saw us together afterward. They guessed we were old friends."

"So I was right. We *were* being followed that night," Jason said, remembering how the hairs had stood up on his neck.

"When you'd left they offered me money to get her into town without you. I said no, honest I did."

"Good of you," Jason observed coldly.

"But they kept coming back, offering me more and more. I couldn't keep saying no. I couldn't afford to."

"So you invited her to lunch that day. No wonder you were annoyed that I came, too."

"No, I wasn't. I was glad really. I never meant her any harm. I didn't want to do it, but I'm on my beam-ends. And then when I saw you yesterday and you said you were going—"

"That's enough," Jason interrupted harshly. The thought of his own part in this was something he would face later, when he could bear it. "So you called your accomplices and told them the chance had come. Then you called Faye and asked her to meet you. You knew she'd agree because she'd never turn down a friend's plea for help. And they were waiting for her."

"It ain't my fault," Luther sniffed tearfully. "I'm fond of Faye but I'm getting old and scared. I used to be a star. Look at me now. Playing a ruddy crocodile. And soon I won't even be able to do that. I ain't got a penny saved."

"No, you blew it all on the horses, didn't you?"

"They won't harm her, honest. They'll just keep her until that rich fiancé pays up."

"You fool," Jason said savagely. "He isn't her fiancé anymore."

"Oh, God!" Luther whispered. "If they find out she's no use to them—"

"They won't be fussy what they do," Jason finished grimly.

Luther's eyes were fixed on Buck. "Stop him looking at me like that," he pleaded.

"He's memorizing your face for future reference. You see, Luther, if Faye comes to any harm Buck and I will come after you, and when we find you I won't even try to control him. So you'd better tell me all you can about these men."

"I don't know nothing," Luther squealed. "They said their names were Harry and Fred."

"What did they look like?"

"Youngish, tallish. One of them had a moustache, only it didn't grow properly on one side."

"Did they give you any idea who they worked for?"

"They didn't tell me nothing that they didn't have to. They were watching every word."

"Where did you call them?"

"At Mason's Guest House. It's a couple of blocks away. That's all I know. Word of honor."

"Word of *what*?" Jason enquired in a pleasant manner that was more frightening than threats.

"Look, I know what you think of me—"

"No, you don't. If you knew what I thought of you you'd faint dead away. When I remember how she defended you, telling me that you were the most honest man in the world and the kindest..." He was shaken with bitter anger as he remembered that scene, but it was directed at himself. He'd known Luther was bad, yet he'd ended up letting Faye walk into this seedy little crook's trap.

He put a restraining hand on Buck. "Get out," he snapped to Luther.

Luther slid past and beat a hasty retreat down the alley. Jason returned to the car and sought out Mason's Guest House. There a friendly landlady told him that the men he was looking for had registered as Mr. Smith and Mr. Brown, and departed the previous evening, leaving no forwarding address. Jason hadn't really hoped for anything else.

He called Dudley and passed on Luther's description of the men. At the mention of the twisted moustache Dudley became thoughtful. "That sounds familiar. Tell the landlady not to touch their rooms. I'll get the fingerprint boys along."

"Is there any word from Conroy Niall?"

"I managed to talk to him. He's not interested. He says they're not engaged any longer and it's nothing to him what happens to her."

Jason swore violently. He hung up and immediately dialed Conroy's office. He'd half expected that Conroy would refuse to speak to him, but he was put through immediately. His blood ran cold at the note of amusement in Conroy's voice. "I decided it would be more entertaining to talk to you than not," Conroy sneered. "You've heard the news, of course."

"I know that Faye's in danger because of her connection with you. If you have a shred of decency left—"

"But I haven't, and at our last meeting you'd have been the first to say so. Why should you have expected me to be different today?"

Jason took a deep breath. His heart was hammering. "You wanted to marry Faye. You must feel something for her."

"Only hatred," Conroy snapped. A vicious note came into his voice. "I offered her everything and she threw it back at me. Now she's going to learn that no one, man or woman, treats me like that and gets away with it. And you're going to learn it, too. I'm telling you what I told Dudley: she's nothing to me anymore and they won't get a penny out of me."

"I know you won't pay the ransom," Jason grated. "But just let the engagement stand to give us time to find her. Surely even you don't want her death on your conscience?"

"But it wouldn't be on my conscience. *I* haven't kidnapped her. And by refusing to pay up I'm behaving like a good citizen. The police don't like people who pay. It encourages further kidnapping. You should know that."

He did know it. In his days on the force he'd had to plead with distraught families not to yield. How sensible the words had sounded then. How little they meant now when it was his Faye in danger. He knew that if he'd had Conroy's millions he would have handed over every last penny in return for her safety. "Niall, I'm asking you—just keep quiet. Don't say anything that will harm her."

Conroy laughed unpleasantly. "Why should I care what happens to her?" he sneered. "The only thing that linked us was her sense of 'obligation' to me, and *you* destroyed that. Now you can save her. It'll be a small return for the favors she's granted you."

"Listen to me," Jason said savagely. "If Faye doesn't come back alive and well, you'd better start running because I'm coming for you. And when I do I'm going to make you sorry you ever hurt her. I've no doubt you've surrounded yourself with guards, but they won't save you. *Nothing* will save you. If you care for your skin, do what you can to protect her now.''

There was a pause, then Conroy said, ''Your threats don't scare me. I hope the two of you rot.'' He hung up.

Jason slammed down the receiver and stood there gasping as if he'd been running. His face was wet. Jason had a terrible feeling that this time Conroy's hatred was stronger than his fear. He was trembling as he left the phone booth and made his way to the car. He got into it and slumped against the wheel, possessed by cold dread.

His guilt was like a savage animal that gnawed and tore at his vitals. He knew he'd inadvertently set Faye up for this by telling Luther that he was leaving. He dropped his head onto the steering wheel, prey to the first real panic attack of his entire life. It was as though the world had stopped at this terrifying moment, and he hung suspended in a void.

He sat for several minutes, trying to force his head to clear and his limbs to come alive again. But nothing happened. His brain could only encompass one word, her name, over and over; her name, cried out silently with love and longing and despair.

Then he felt an urgent pawing on his arm. He straightened up. Buck was looking at him intently, waiting for a lead, and the sight calmed him. The universe seemed to steady, and he was himself again. ''All right, old fellow. We're not going to let her down.''

He started the car and swung it out into the stream of traffic. In a few minutes they were on the road back to London.

He drove straight to New Scotland Yard and went to find Dudley. The detective was a big man whose face bore a superficial look of bluff heartiness. Only those who got close noticed the chill behind his small, piggy eyes. He let out a grunt of satisfaction at the sight of Jason. "Look at that," he said, pushing a book of photographs over the desk to Jason and stabbing at one of the pictures with a blunt finger.

Jason studied the face. It was mean and sullen, but what struck him sharply was the way the moustache was awry on one side, where a scar had stunted its growth. "Freddie Todd," Dudley announced with satisfaction. "Small-time villain. We've got his fingerprints on file and I faxed them to Cranton. They've just called to say his prints were all over 'Mr. Brown's' room at the guest house."

"So where does that get us?" Jason demanded, suspicious of Dudley's air of suppressed delight.

"If we're lucky it gets *me* Vincent Barker," Dudley declared. "Freddie's been running errands for him lately, and it's my guess he's behind this."

Jason tried not to let his inner disturbance show. Vincent Barker was a shadowy presence behind a good deal of major crime, but he maintained his distance with such skill and ruthlessness that no policeman had yet succeeded in laying anything at his door. Twice he'd almost been within the grasp of the law, and both times vital witnesses had vanished without a trace. He was a man who believed in killing as a routine precaution. Dudley was almost slavering at the prospect of a chance to nail him, but Jason's fear was increased a hundredfold. "I spoke to Niall," he began to say.

"That was out of line," Dudley interrupted sharply. "You seem to forget you don't belong here anymore. I called you because you can be useful, but don't push it. What did he say?"

"The same as before. The engagement's off and he doesn't care if they find out."

Dudley shrugged. "They probably know already. She'll have told them herself."

"Why should she?"

"She's alone, isn't she? She'll be too scared to think straight. She'll probably think that if she tells them it's off they'll let her go."

"Instead they'll kill her," Jason shouted.

"Look, the one thing I can't afford on this case is sentiment. Naturally I'll do all I can to get her out alive, but we have to face facts. The chances are against it."

Jason resisted the temptation to plant his fist in the center of Dudley's complacent face, and said, as calmly as he could, "If you rescue her alive it looks good on your record."

"Sure. But it also looks good if I get Barker. This is where you can help me. I need people who are going to talk and the usual underworld informers have clammed up. But they may talk to you because you were chucked out." He gave Jason a sly look. "Do it right and you could work your way back."

His mind preoccupied with thoughts of Faye, Jason didn't immediately take in Dudley's meaning. Then it dawned on him that he was being offered a chance to salvage his career with the police. "What do you mean, 'do it right'?" he demanded.

"I mean no going solo," Dudley snapped, his eyes hard. "Anything you find out, you turn over to me. One or two people think you were hard done by. If I put in a good word I'm pretty sure you would be taken back."

It was the thing Jason had wanted more than anything on earth, an end to his present futile, rootless existence. Now he knew it meant nothing, for without Faye his life would be desolate. And leaving everything to Dudley meant abandoning Faye to the mercy of this hard man's ambition, for whatever formal words Dudley might utter about the safety of the victim he would be just as pleased to make his arrests for murder as for kidnapping.

Jason returned to the car, his mind churning with a hundred tormented thoughts. One phrase kept echoing: Dudley had said, "She's alone, isn't she?" and now Jason understood how alone she truly was. Luther, whom she'd thought of as a friend, had betrayed her. Conroy was openly rejoicing in her trouble. Dudley, who should have been concerned for her life, was indifferent as long as he made a good arrest. Her father had been well-meaning but foolish, throwing onto her shoulders the whole burden of their misfortune.

Pictures came before him, illuminated so searingly that he wondered how he'd missed their significance until now. When they'd arrived at Haverill Manor, Alaric had tried to climb the steps alone. He'd tottered and instantly Faye had been there, supporting him. Jason remembered the way she'd almost failed under his weight, but then braced herself to bear it. Their whole relationship had been summed up in that moment.

He remembered her trapped on the ladder in the library, holding on to him and saying beseechingly, "You're the only one I *can* trust... if it wasn't for that..." And now he, too, had let her down.

She'd put her faith in him, and if in her desperation, she'd used unorthodox methods, what right had he to blame her for that? Another memory rose to torment him, more bitter than all the other's: Faye, her voice full of passionate intensity, saying, "If you love someone enough, nothing else matters. You can overlook anything even if—even if you think it's terribly wrong. Perhaps that's what love is—understanding when you don't really understand at all."

He hadn't even tried to understand. Instead he'd raged at her in bitter anger and disillusion, in a way that now seemed to him nothing more than selfish hypocrisy. And in the end he'd betrayed her, even if innocently. He had no right to hope for her forgiveness, but that hardly mattered now, if only he got her back. If he was given that miracle he would be content to live on the fringe of her life, loving her and asking nothing but to see her and know she was safe.

The streets were getting shabbier as he drove. At last he drew up outside an unprepossessing little pub, and he and Buck got out. It was early evening and the bar was only sparsely occupied, but the man he was looking for was always one of the first to arrive. There was no sign of him yet, however, and Jason went quietly up to the bar to order soda water, a brown ale and some water for Buck. Then he seated himself where he could see the door and waited, hardly able to contain his impatience.

He didn't have to wait long. After five minutes a thin man sidled through the door and up to the bar. Sidling seemed to be his natural movement. "You're late tonight, Ferris," Jason called.

Ferris jumped half out of his skin. When he saw who it was his features registered a mixture of amiability and caution. "Mr. Royce, ain't seen you in a long time."

Jason indicated the brown ale. "I remembered what you drink. Sit down. And stop looking so nervous. I'm out of the force now."

"Yeah, I heard. But there ain't no one who believes you were bent."

"Thanks. I wish my ex-colleagues agreed with you. Just for the record, are you keeping on the straight and narrow these days?"

"Sort of," Ferris said carefully. "You know how it is . . ."

"Yes, I know. I'm not here to hound you. I want some information, and yours was always the best." Ferris's small-time villainy had never earned him enough to keep him in beer, so he supplemented his fortunes by informing. "What can you tell me about Vincent Barker these days?"

Ferris paled. "I don't have nothing to do with him, and I don't want to," he said hastily.

"I know that, but you know what's going on. I want anything you've heard, any gossip, no matter how small, *anything*."

His pallor and the tension in his face made Ferris look at him, startled. "It really matters, then?"

"Yes," Jason said bleakly. "It really matters."

"The only thing I've heard on the grapevine is that one or two of his blokes have been using an old empty warehouse recently. Some say they're storing explosives there. Some say they're converting stolen vehicles for a big job. Nobody really knows."

"Exactly where is this place?"

"On Nabel Street, near the docks. That's all I know, honest."

"Fine." Jason pushed some money into his hands. "Take care of yourself, Ferris."

He hurried back to the car. Before he started up he thrust his hand into the glove compartment and drew out a gun. He studied it for a moment before deciding it wasn't big enough for this job. He had a more powerful weapon in his apartment and it would be worth making a detour. He drove home as fast as he dared and was just retrieving the other gun from his safe when the phone rang.

It was Dudley. "Have you discovered anything?" he barked.

Jason thought fast before saying, "Not a thing. They won't talk to me, either." He wasn't going to risk Dudley charging all over the situation.

Dudley laughed grimly. "Well, if you do learn anything, don't try any stupid, independent stuff. Faye Stafford is dead."

Jason's heart lurched. The world stopped and everything turned black. He wanted to scream, but the only sound that came out was a hoarse croak. "Dead?"

"As good as. The evening newspapers have just come out. Niall's splashed himself all over the headlines, denying any engagement. If she isn't dead now she will be as soon as they read that."

"The bastard," Jason whispered.

"Just you remember what I said. Don't waste your time on her. She's as good as dead."

Chapter Fourteen

Faye had arrived at the pizza house on Elvin Street to find Luther waiting outside on the pavement. "Come on," he'd said, looking down and taking her arm.

"Aren't we going inside?"

"No, it's best if we—look, if we just go down that street..." He was urging her on as he spoke, his hand firmly grasping her arm.

She'd noticed his embarrassment but she couldn't guess the real cause. He hurried her away from the main road and down a deserted side street. "Here we are," he said, coming abreast of a car.

She stared at the car, wondering how the down-at-heel Luther could be associated with this sleek, new Jaguar. Then she noticed that the rear windows were blacked out and at the same moment it suddenly seemed ominous that Luther hadn't met her eyes.

But before her whirling brain could make the connection the rear door opened and a man reached out and seized her roughly. At his touch all her lightning reflexes came into play. She fought well, using her dancer's strength and forcing her assailant to get half out of the car to hold on to her.

She heard him yell to Luther, "Help me," but Luther was backing away, eyes wide with horror. As he reached the corner the man yelled again but his words were choked off as Faye kicked him in the groin. He howled with pain but held on to her doggedly and before she could kick him again, another man got out of the front to help him. Between them they overpowered Faye and manhandled her into the back of the car. She fell to the floor and by the time she got up they were moving.

She hurled herself at the door but it was locked and all her frantic efforts wouldn't open it. While she was tugging the handle the man reached over and grabbed her again, pulling her back against the seat. "Stop that!" he yelled. "You can't open it so don't waste your time."

She swung her arm so fast he never saw it and clouted him across the eyes. He screamed and drew back his fist to hit her. *"That's enough,"* snapped the driver who'd seen the whole thing in his rearview mirror. "Our orders are not to hurt her."

The man in the back seat managed to get both his arms around Faye and held her in a viselike grip. His face was close to hers and she could see his unhealthy expression and the odd twisted way his moustache grew on one side. "How do I stop this wildcat from hurting *me*?" he growled.

Faye answered by spitting in his face. The next minute she was being shaken like a rag doll. Her head ached and the little dark world where she was trapped spun around giddily and the man that held her tied her hands behind her back and thrust her against the seat where she lay in a state of near collapse, her heart hammering wildly.

"I said don't hurt her," the driver shouted over his shoulder. "Those were the orders."

"Then Mr. Barker should try coping with her himself," her other kidnapper snapped.

"Don't ever say that name," the driver snapped suddenly. "Forget you ever heard of him. And you—" his eyes flicked to Faye in the mirror "—just keep quiet and you'll be all right. As soon as Niall pays up you can go—assuming he thinks you're worth half a million."

"Half a—?" Faye took a deep breath and forced herself to speak normally. "I hope he has more sense than to pay a penny."

The driver grinned. "That would be a pity. If you can't be converted to cash you're worthless."

A shiver went through Faye. She knew Conroy wouldn't pay ransom for her now, and she'd come perilously close to blurting out the truth. Whoever "Mr. Barker" was, his own men were terrified of him, and he would order her disposal without compunction. Her only hope lay in keeping quiet and seeking a chance to escape. But as if reading her mind the driver ordered, "Cover her up, Fred. The less she knows the better."

In a moment Fred had pulled her sideways until she was almost stretched out on the seat, and tossed a blanket over her and wrapped it so she couldn't move. "Don't give me any more trouble," he warned.

Now she had no idea where they were going. She could tell the car was traveling at great speed and occasionally she felt it lurch sideways as they took a bend. Time passed and still they traveled, and she guessed she was being taken to London.

At last the car came to a halt and the rear door opened. She sensed someone reaching inside, then rough male hands grabbed her and pulled her out into the street. At first her cramped legs refused to support her and she staggered, but her captor gripped her harder, holding her upright and forcing her to walk forward. She was still covered in the blanket and had no idea where she was going. She tripped on some steps and the man's fingers dug deeper into her arm to stop her from falling. There was the confused sound of voices. Someone snapped, "Hurry up, we ain't got all night." Then she was moving again, and a door slammed. It made a jangly noise, like an elevator door, and a moment later she was going upward.

From the sounds of clanking she guessed she was in an ancient elevator, probably in a building that had fallen into disuse. She was afraid of elevators, especially old ones, and for a moment the thought of being stranded here with these evil men almost made her scream, but she forced herself to stay silent. If she had nothing else she still had her pride and it would have to sustain her through the dreadful time to come.

She tried to work out how many floors up they were going, but she was too disoriented. At last the lift jerked to a halt, the door jangled again and she was marched out and onward for a few yards. Then they stopped. Another door. The sound of it opening. And a push in her back that sent her sprawling onto the floor. Before she could get up she heard the door slam again and a key turn in the lock.

She wiggled out from under the blanket, thankful to be free of its dreadful heat. A narrow iron bed stood in the corner. She made her way to it stiffly and sat down on the edge. Her head was swimming and her hands were still tied. Somewhere, deep down, a wilderness of fear was waiting to swamp her, but she refused to give in to it.

The most terrible thought was of Alaric, waiting for her return, growing more fearful until his heart couldn't stand the burden. She got up, painfully made her way to the door and kicked it. When there was no answer she kicked harder.

"Shut up!" a male voice replied. "That won't do you any good."

Faye hammered again and suddenly the door was flung open. The man who'd driven the car stood there. "Did you hear me tell you to shut up?" he demanded menacingly.

"I want to make a phone call," she said.

He laughed mirthlessly, and called to someone outside. "D'you hear that? The prisoner wants to make a phone call. Every prisoner is entitled to one call, that's the law, ain't it?" His laughter stopped abruptly and he seized her arm with fingers that dug into her until they hurt. "Only not here, darlin'. Here you ain't got no rights except to keep quiet and do as you're told. Okay?"

His nearness was sickening but Faye forced herself to look at him and speak calmly. "I just want to speak to my father and tell him I'm all right. What harm can there be in that?"

He grinned. "You reckon you're all right? Like it here, do you? Like to stay?" He laughed at the look of revulsion on her face. "Your dad will know what's happened by now. Someone will have made a call."

"Yes but he's got a weak heart. *Please*, let me speak to him myself," Faye begged desperately.

"And have you sending him coded messages. You must think I was born yesterday." He thrust her back against the wall and walked out.

With the lithe ability of a dancer, Faye managed to bring her hands forward and slip free of the make-shift bonds, though her wrists were raw from the rope. She returned to the bed and sat on it, trying not to give in to despair. At last she raised her head and looked around the room that was her prison. It was dirty and depressing, with a tiled floor. The only furniture was the narrow bed, one chair and a table. There was one other door, and when she tried it Faye found it led to a small washroom, with one tiny window.

The window in the main room was larger, and she found she could open it, but there was a metal grid on the outside. It looked new, as though someone had recently prepared this place to receive her. The spaces were large enough for her to get an arm through, but nothing more, and they gave a tantalizing sense that freedom was only a few inches away. She pressed against the metal, trying to see as much as possible. The building formed four sides of a square. Her window was on the inside, and looked out onto a shaft containing fire escapes. Faye studied the fire escape opposite and saw that it was full of gaps. By squinting upward she could make out a patch of rapidly darkening sky.

The door leading to the passage opened and the same man as before came in with a tray. He grinned when he saw her. "Having a good look are you? Look all you like. It won't help. We're five floors up and the fire escape doesn't go all the way down. Here's your supper. My name's Harry if you want to be sociable."

Faye looked at him in hate-filled silence.

Harry shrugged. "Please yourself." He set down the tray and departed.

"Supper" was a stale meat pie and a plastic cup of instant coffee that tasted as if it had been made with water from a hot tap. After one sip Faye pulled a face and decided to do without.

Now she needed all the discipline she'd ever learned in her career. The confinement was bad enough to someone used to wide spaces, but the mental anguish was a thousand times worse.

Jason had been right about Luther all the time. She'd trusted her old friend, overlooking the signs of weakness. But how *could* she ever have suspected him? It was Luther who'd been a second father to her. Only Jason had seen further. Wainright had set him up, and he'd suffered exactly the same sense of betrayal that tortured her now. After that he'd known better than to trust anyone.

But then she had come along and he'd loved and trusted her. The discovery of the truth had struck a blow at an already wounded man. She couldn't blame him for leaving her as he had, but a corner of her heart obstinately refused to believe he would abandon her now.

And yet, suppose he didn't know what had happened? If that were true, Faye knew she would be dead soon.

She called on all the techniques she'd learned to battle stage fright. Take deep, calming breaths, refuse to look past the next few minutes. Concentrate one step ahead, get that right, then the next. This wasn't really so different. She would have to play it by ear, take every moment as it came, and pray that somewhere Jason could hear her heart crying out to him.

She delayed lying down on the greasy-looking bed as long as possible, but at last weariness claimed her and she stretched out. When she awoke it was light and the door was opening. Harry came in with another tray bearing an equally unappetizing meal. Faye slid her left hand beneath the blanket so that he couldn't see that she wore no ring and watched him in silence.

"No news from Niall yet," he observed to no one in particular. "Seems you're engaged to a very elusive gentleman. Pity, that. Pity for you I mean."

He grinned and regarded her hopefully to see if she could be goaded into speech. But Faye said nothing and after a while he shrugged, disappointed, and walked out, locking the door behind him.

The day that followed was dreadful. There was nothing to do but look at the four blank walls and follow the same interminable thoughts like a mouse on a treadmill. Every sound from beyond the door was ominous. From somewhere at the far end of the corridor she could hear the voices of her two captors having an argument, but sounding bored at the same time.

She was listening for a third voice, a phone bell, or maybe a radio, something from the outside world that would tell them Conroy had disowned her. She knew it would come soon. Then there would be a silence while they looked at her door, then at each other, wondering which one of them should kill her. The thought made her stretch her legs and flex her feet, hoping that her recent practice sessions had left her in good shape. She had a kick like a mule, and at least one of them was going to feel it, she promised herself.

Over long, slow hours she watched the patch of light move around the room until at last it faded completely. The day had left her exhausted and as darkness fell she lay down, expecting to sleep at once, but immediately found herself alert and wakeful. If she had to spend the night counting hours as she'd spent the day she might go mad.

Suddenly she grew tense and still. She'd heard something, not from the corridor but from outside the window. She sat up, straining her ears, praying that she wasn't suffering delusions. But the sound came again, and this time there was no mistake; someone was on the fire escape.

Moving as quietly as she could she slid out of bed and crept to the window. In the pale moonlight she could just make out the silhouette of a tall man. Hardly daring to hope, she pulled the window open, then smothered a cry of joy at the sight of Jason. He put his finger to his lips and shook his head.

Faye pressed very close to the grid. "Darling," she whispered. She wanted to laugh and shout for joy at the sight of him.

He reached in through the grid and touched her face. "I was afraid I'd never see you again." He curved his hand around her head, drawing her closer until he could brush his lips against her. For a moment all danger ceased to exist in the joy of being with him again, feeling his love encompass her. "Have they hurt you?" he murmured.

"I'm all right. Jason, my father—"

"Bearing up well," he said hastily. "He'll be fine when he sees you safe. But first I have to unbolt this grid and it's going to take time. Go listen at the door. If you hear anyone coming signal me, shut the window and lie down. And take this." He handed her a pistol. "Conroy has publicly disowned you. It can't be long now before they decide you're no use to them, and you may have to use it."

She took the weapon gingerly and crept over to the door, straining her ears for a noise from the other side. But there was nothing. By contrast the faint sounds Jason made as he worked on the grid sounded terrifyingly loud, and at any moment she expected to hear someone approaching.

After a long time she thought she heard footsteps approaching the door from the end of a long passage. She hurried back to pull the window open. Jason was struggling with a bolt that seemed to be stiff, gasping with the effort. "I think someone's coming," she whispered.

"This is the last one but it won't budge," he said desperately. "Dear God, just a few more moments."

The steps were much closer. Faye shut the window and lay down in the bed with the gun concealed beneath the blanket. There was the sound of a key in the lock, then the door swung open. Harry switched on the light and stood there with a copy of the evening paper in his hand. Faye saw the headline: IT'S ALL OFF, SAYS NIALL. Harry was smiling with sickening pleasure. "It would seem that you have a bit of a problem," he said. "Niall says you're not worth a penny to him. Know where he is now? On a plane to the Bahamas. He can't be contacted."

Faye never took her eyes from him. She knew that everything depended on the next few moments. Harry locked the door behind him. "Now we won't be disturbed," he said softly. "If you're not valuable there's only one thing to be done with you. But we can let that wait until morning. If you're not useful in one way, you can be in another."

He began to approach the bed, unbuckling his belt as he moved. With a calmness that belied her inner trembling Faye lifted her hand over the blanket, pointed the gun at his chest and said, "Not another step."

Harry stared in disbelief. "Where did you get that?" he demanded. "You didn't have it before."

"But I have it now," she said quietly, "and I'll use it before I'll let you lay a finger on me."

He took a tentative step forward. Faye raised the gun, but to her dismay she saw his face brighten. "You've never held one of those things before," he said. "You hold it as though you were hoping it wouldn't go off. Go on, use it, if you dare."

He began to walk forward again. Faye flattened herself against the wall, wondering if she could bring herself to shoot him.

But at the last minute he stopped. Glancing sideways she saw what he had seen, the window swinging wide to reveal Jason standing there with the grid gone, his face dark with rage. The next second Harry had launched himself toward her, reaching for the gun. She swung it wide but it jerked as he seized her wrist, and discharged into the wall. The sound was deafening in the little room. The next moment Harry was reeling back under a hammer blow from Jason's fist. He landed on the floor and lay there in a daze. Jason moved quickly to stand over him. "Get out, quickly," he told her.

"But you—"

"The shot will have roused them. They'll all be here in a minute." He took the gun. "I can keep them off with this."

"No, come with me. I can't leave you here."

"Faye, I haven't time to argue, *please* do it my way. The fire escape goes down two floors. You have to go down the rest by the rope I've left attached." Still training the gun on Harry he pulled her hard against him for a brief kiss. "Now hurry," he said tersely.

Reluctantly she climbed out onto the fire escape and began to run down. As Jason had said the stairs ended abruptly after two floors, but there was the rope. He'd tied it around one of the corner supports and it looked secure enough, but it swung right over the drop. Faye peered down the remaining floors but all she could see was the rope vanishing into the darkness. Her stomach churned at the thought of launching herself into that void, but she had no choice.

She climbed over the rail and began to move gingerly down the rope. Soon she was below the level of the metal landing, then down farther, into the darkness. The rope swayed as she descended, and she knew that if Jason hadn't restored her confidence she would never have been able to make it.

Now she was level with the third floor. Just a little further to go.

But suddenly a light came on behind a second-floor window on the far side. The next second a man had opened it and leaned out. He was carrying a gun that he raised and aimed directly at Faye. She was above him and the only escape lay past him. She was still too high to drop. Nothing could save her now.

But instead of the noise of a shot there came a soft, menacing snarl from somewhere in the gloom. The man looked around, puzzled, and the snarl came again. He aimed in the general direction of the sound. Faye held her breath. She could just make out Buck, who had come up the stairs as far as he could, stopping where they had disintegrated on the second floor. He was level with the gunman and had to be able to see the gun in the light from the window. For a long moment nothing moved, and the gunman seemed to decide he had nothing to fear. He swung back to Faye and raised the weapon again.

But before he could fire, a shape seemed to gather itself together in the shadows and go flying through the air. The man screamed at the sight of Buck's eyes, burning with hate, rushing toward him. He flung up an arm to defend himself and felt a pair of fangs enclose it. The next moment he'd fallen from the window ledge, screaming again as he plunged to the ground with Buck hanging on.

There were shouts from below. Lights. A powerful torch played over Faye and a man called, "Police. Come on down."

Faye shinnied down the rest of the rope. She jumped the last few feet and was caught by a heavily built man. "Chief Inspector Dudley," he said. "I take it you're Faye Stafford?"

"Yes, but never mind that. You've got to help Jason. He's still up there—"

"Isn't that him coming down now?" Dudley asked, following the torch's beam. Faye looked up and cried out with joy at the sight of Jason descending the rope. "I guessed he'd try a crazy stunt like this," Dudley added, "so I had a man watching his apartment. When he came here I followed."

Faye hardly heard him. Her eyes were fixed on Jason, getting nearer. As he landed she reached for him and he pulled her into his arms. They clung together, neither capable of words, or needing them. In that long moment of silence everything was said.

"Can you save that until later?" Dudley demanded tersely. "What's been going on?"

"You'll find two more of them on the top floor," Jason told him. "Don't bother to hurry. They won't be moving for a while."

Dudley disappeared with two men. The little yard seemed full of policemen. One of them was kneeling by the gunman and radioing for an ambulance. Beside him lay Buck, not moving. With an exclamation of distress Faye dropped to her knees beside the dog's still form and stroked his face. To her relief she felt the rasp of Buck's tongue licking her hand, but it was frighteningly feeble.

The policeman had finished asking for the ambulance. Now he added, "And we need a veterinary ambulance, too." He ran his eyes over Buck and added, "Better tell them to hurry."

Faye and Jason were seated together in a waiting room at the animal hospital, their hands entwined. Faye had called Alaric to assure him of her safety, then returned to Jason to wait while Buck was taken care of. "He did it," she whispered. "He outfaced that gun. He finally found the key."

"Of course," Jason agreed. "The key was *you* all the time. You're the key to everything. Buck knew that before I did."

He drew her against him and they sat in silence while another hour ticked by. Then the vet emerged, briskly stripping off his gloves. They rose and looked at him tensely. "Fine!" he said. "None of the broken ribs pierced a lung. Give him a little time and he'll be back in top form."

Jason and Faye threw themselves into each other's arms, speechless with joy. Eventually Jason said, "I think we should go see Dudley at the station. We ought to have gone there first. By now he'll be chewing the carpet."

He was right. Dudley eyed them coldly. "Nice of you two to get here at last," he said. "Where the hell have you been?"

"We had to check up on our friend first," Jason said. "You'll be relieved to know that he's going to be fine."

"Ah, yes, that dog." Dudley's eyes narrowed. "I seem to recall that a police dog vanished mysteriously about the time you left the force. He'd been designated dangerous and was due to be put down."

A chill went through Faye at this unexpected threat, but a squeeze from Jason's hand held her silent. "If I'm not mistaken," he said, "the man he brought down was Vincent Barker's right-hand man. Quite a coup for you."

"Except that I won't get any credit," Dudley said sourly. "You had no right to take off like that on your own. But of course what really concerned you was snatching all the kudos and returning to the force in a blaze of glory."

"No, what concerned me was Faye's life," Jason said. "I don't want to come back to the force. *Come back?* To people who treated me the way they did just because they wanted everything swept under the carpet? Come crawling back as if I was grateful for being kicked in the teeth?"

"I wonder if you'll still say that when the compliments are being handed out," Dudley snapped.

"But the compliments will come to you when it's known I was acting under your orders," Jason observed.

Dudley eyed him suspiciously. "Under my orders?"

"The master plan was yours. I merely obeyed instructions. You could get a commendation—if I say the right things."

Their eyes held. Dudley's fell first. "Well, I'm not a dog expert," he muttered. "Alsatians all look the same to me."

"Exactly."

Dudley coughed awkwardly. "Now Miss Stafford, I'll start with your statement."

At last it was all over and they were out in the street. Faye stared at him in wonder. "You could have had your career back, and you gave it up for Buck."

"Not just for Buck. Faye, I'm *free*. It would always have been wrong for me to return, but until recently I'd have done it because the force was all I had. Not now, though. Don't you see? I have—" He stopped and looked at her, then seized her in his arms and kissed her.

At last he released her and searched her face anxiously. "What do I have, Faye? No, don't answer yet. There's something I have to tell you first." He met her clear, candid eyes and knew that this was going to be the most difficult confession of his life. "All this was my fault. I bumped into Luther in town and told him I was leaving. *I* was the one who really betrayed you. Because of my pride and stupidity you could have died."

She laid a reassuring hand over his mouth. He kissed her fingers then went on determinedly, "You once said 'if you love someone enough, nothing else matters. You can overlook anything, even if you think it's terribly wrong.' You did mean it, didn't you, Faye?"

"I know that nothing could make me stop loving you. Jason, let's forget the past. We each have things to forgive. All that matters now is the future."

"Aren't you worried about what kind of future?"

"No. Next week you'll get a brilliant assignment that'll make your name. And I'm going to contact an agent who once told me to look him up if I ever left the Kramer Ballet." She squeezed his hand. "We're going places together."

He took her face between his hands. "I don't deserve you," he said, moved, "but by God I'm *going* to deserve you." He touched her lips gently, then asked, "But how will your father feel when he knows we're going to be married?"

"He already knows. I told him when I called from the vet hospital. He said, 'It's all right now, isn't it, darling?' I said it's very much all right. Oh, darling—darling, we can't do this in the middle of the street. We're causing an obstruction."

"Then they'll just have to move around us," Jason said, bending his head for a very thorough and satisfying kiss.

* * * * *

Silhouette Romance®

AWARD OF EXCELLENCE

LONG, TALL TEXANS

Diana Palmer brings you the second Award of Excellence title
SUTTON'S WAY

In Diana Palmer's bestselling Long, Tall Texans trilogy, you had a mesmerizing glimpse of Quinn Sutton—a mean, lean Wyoming wildcat of a man, with a disposition to match.

Now, in September, Quinn's back with a story of his own. Set in the Wyoming wilderness, he learns a few things about women from snowbound beauty Amanda Callaway—and a lot more about love.

He's a Texan at heart . . . who soon has a Wyoming wedding in mind!

The Award of Excellence is given to one specially selected title per month. Spend September discovering *Sutton's Way* #670 . . . only in Silhouette Romance.

RS670-1R

You'll flip . . . your pages won't!
Read paperbacks *hands-free* with

Book Mate • I

The perfect "mate" for all your romance paperbacks

Traveling • Vacationing • At Work • In Bed • Studying • Cooking • Eating

Perfect size for all standard paperbacks, this wonderful invention makes reading a pure pleasure! Ingenious design holds paperback books OPEN and FLAT so even wind can't ruffle pages— leaves your hands free to do other things. Reinforced, wipe-clean vinyl-covered holder flexes to let you turn pages without undoing the strap . . . supports paperbacks so well, they have the strength of hardcovers!

Pages turn WITHOUT opening the strap

SEE-THROUGH STRAP

Reinforced back stays flat

Built in bookmark

BOOK MARK

BACK COVER HOLDING STRIP

10 x 7¼ opened
Snaps closed for easy carrying, too

JOIN TOP-SELLING AUTHOR
EMILIE RICHARDS
FOR A SPECIAL ANNIVERSARY

Only in September, and
only in Silhouette
Romance, we'll be bringing
you Emilie's twentieth
Silhouette novel,
Island Glory (SR #675).

Island Glory brings back
Glory Kalia, who made her
first—and very
memorable—appearance in
Aloha Always (SR #520).
Now she's here with a
story—and a hero—of her
own. Thrill to warm
tropical nights with Glory
and Jared Farrell, a man
who doesn't want to give
any woman his heart but
quickly learns that, with
Glory, he has no choice.

Join Silhouette Romance
now and experience a taste
of *Island Glory*.

FOUR UNIQUE SERIES
FOR EVERY WOMAN YOU ARE...

Silhouette Romance

Love, at its most tender, provocative, emotional... in stories that will make you laugh and cry while bringing you the magic of falling in love.

Silhouette Special Edition

Sophisticated, substantial and packed with emotion, these powerful novels of life and love will capture your imagination and steal your heart.

Silhouette Desire

Open the door to romance and passion. Humorous, emotional, compelling—yet always a believable and sensuous story—Silhouette Desire never fails to deliver on the promise of love.

Silhouette Intimate Moments

Enter a world of excitement, of romance heightened by suspense, adventure and the passions every woman dreams of. Let us sweep you away.